THE TERRITORY

SARAH GOVETT

Firefly

for Noa and Alba

First published in 2015
by Firefly Press
25 Gabalfa Road, Llandaff North, Cardiff, CF14 2JJ
www.fireflypress.co.uk

Reprinted 2016 and 2017

This edition 2018

A CIP catalogue record of this book is available from the British Library.

Print ISBN 9781910080184
epub ISBN 9781910080191

This book has been published with the support of the Welsh Books Council.

Typeset by: Elaine Sharples

Printed and bound by: PULSIO SARL

My name's Noa Blake. Yes, that's Noah without an 'h'. Yes, it's a real girl's name. Apparently Noa means *movement* in Hebrew, and I moved a lot in the womb. And now. I've only heard of one other Noa – my godmother's best friend's daughter. She flunked her TAA last year, so now she's a Fish.

New Year's Resolution 2059: Pass TAA and don't become a Fish.

Uncle Pete told Mum there's an 85 per cent chance that I'll become a Fish. He didn't say 'Fish' obviously. He said 'Wetlands Citizen' in that weird, nasally voice of his, as if there was something stuck up his nostril. (A cobnut probably. Uncle Pete's always eating cobnuts, the roasted, salted type. His breath stinks of them.) It's because I'm a Norm, he said. If Mum and Dad had actually listened to him fifteen years ago 'rather than acting like mindless hippies' and paid for the 'enhancement programme', I'd be a Childe and there would be a 99.5 per cent chance that I'd pass my TAA and be able to stay in the Territory.

I couldn't hear the rest of the conversation. When Mum saw me listening at the door, she did her funny look, wrinkling up her forehead like detailed shading in Art. I'm so malc at Art. She shut the door and all I could hear then was:

Mum: 'Mumble mumble mumble … how could you … mumble mumble mumble … she's clever enough …. mumble mumble mumble … never forgive.'

Uncle Pete: Whine whine whine … she has a right to know … whine whine whine … you need to prepare yourself … whine whine whine … you could speak to someone in the Ministry … whine whine whine … late upgrade.'

Then Mum started to cry so I went upstairs. When she cries, Mum 'needs to be alone'.

I'm pleased I'm a Norm not some freakoid Childe though.

Today's assembly was about sacrifice. Yawn. Loads of assemblies are about sacrifice at the moment. It's THE topic of Mr Daniels. I doubt he's ever had to sacrifice anything – apart from his hair. I can't think of him without seeing his shiny, bald, fat head with its squirrel's tail of grey clinging desperately to the sides.

Anyway, he was going on about Species Day or 'Dead Dog Day' as Jack and I call it. About how it had been necessary for the survival of the Territory that we put our species first and kill all the pets so they stopped using up our food. Of course he didn't put it quite like that, but that's the basic gist. We were then supposed to reflect in silence for five minutes about difficult and important decisions and how we grow from them.

It was weird looking round the hall during the silence. Most of the freakoids had their heads bowed. Jack was picking his nose (he can be grim) and Daisy was practising raising one eyebrow. I'd learnt to do this last week and Daisy thought it looked cool. A couple of other Norms my age were struggling not to cry as the memories came back. To cry would be BAD. Deduction of a point from your TAA score BAD, and then, before you know it, 'Hello Fish Face'. The strangest thing was looking at the blank faces of the youngest pupils. They had been born after Species Day so didn't have a clue what it meant to have a dog or a cat as a friend. To feed him, stroke him, play with him and then have THEM come along and take him away.

I'll never forget that Saturday. I was seven. Jack and I had been playing fetch with Rex in the street all afternoon. Jack didn't have his own dog as his mum thought they smelt bad and wasn't prepared to pick up their poo in plastic bags, so he always played with mine, and Rex ended up sort of being half his. I remember it starting to rain. The raindrops were massive and soaked through my clothes and started literally dripping off Jack's nose so he looked ridiculous. Rex's normally long hair was plastered to his skin so he seemed loads smaller, as if he had shrunk in the wash. I hugged Jack goodbye and sprinted up the stairs to my flat, Rex bouncing along at my heels. I knew something was wrong as soon as I saw Mum. She was standing in the kitchen with a white face, red eyes and a really straight back. And she didn't even mention the muddy trail that Rex and I had made. She talked fast, too fast. I didn't understand at first, didn't want to. Because of her job at the Laboratory, she'd been given advance warning. That night at 9pm the police were going to round up all the pets in the Territory and kill them. No one was supposed to know so that they wouldn't be tempted to hide them or resist. The police would get to keep their attack dogs, of course. The rules never applied to them.

I asked Mum what the plan was. She's always been the boss in our family as far as organising and planning stuff goes. Dad's a bit malc at stuff like that.

'Where are we going to hide Rex?' I whispered. 'He could live under my bed. Or in the gap behind the washing machine. They won't find him there. Jack didn't even find me there when we were playing hide and seek and he's really good at looking.'

Mum pursed her lips. 'We're not going to hide Rex. They'd find him and then that'd mean…'

'What?'

'Nothing. We're just going to say goodbye to Rex ourselves. Take responsibility.' Her voice trailed off.

We waited until Dad got home from work just after 7. We gave Rex the meat we would have had for dinner, hugged him as hard as he'd let us and then sang the 'Rex is Cool' song that Dad had invented and that always made Rex's tail thud on the floor in approval. In the middle of the third verse, Mum hit him over the head with a cricket bat and he made a quiet whimper and then was silent.

We handed Rex's body to the police when they came and they wouldn't look me in the eye.

We had double Art today. Mrs Foster got us to draw a picture of something that represented someone we knew. Most of the class, the freakoids especially, looked massively confused. All term we had been doing these well boring scale drawings of buildings and stuff, to train us up to be 'useful' architects and engineers instead of 'mere' painters, so this was a bit of a shock. Hugo Barnes stood up and asked whether we should check with Mr Daniels if this was on the curriculum, but Mrs Foster just raised one eyebrow and gave him such an evil glare that he shrank back onto his stool. Daisy and I spent the next few minutes raising eyebrows at one another in celebration.

Anyway, most drawings were typically limp. Amanda, who spends 80 per cent of her freakoid brain obsessing over Hugo and the other 20 per cent deciding how best to draw attention to her non-existent boobs, stayed true to form and completely failed to understand the task. She drew a picture of her brother to represent, wait for it: her brother (durr!!) If you can't upload it… I can't believe she'll probably pass her TAA. I mean, the whole point is it's supposed to keep the best brains in the Territory.

I drew a picture of a blanket to represent my mum. I explained to Mrs Foster that this was because Mum's always there to comfort me and wrap her arms around me. Jack and Daisy both mimed puking, but I think Mrs Foster must have liked what I said because although, as usual, my drawing sucked, I actually got 80 per cent this time.

You should have seen Jack's drawing though. Jack is ACE at Art. He did a charcoal sketch of a dog chained to a post. It was supposed to represent his dad. The dimensions were all a bit off, in the way that only people who are properly good at Art can pull off, but the eyes just stared back at you in a really haunting way. Black, with dots of soul at the centre. What was so weird was that the picture was exactly like Jack's dad. Not exactly like him obviously, 'cos he's not a dog, but at the same time just like him. I think it seemed so shocking as you just don't see pictures of dogs anymore, not anywhere. Not since Dead Dog Day. And because Jack's dad was a Subversive. No one mentions them either. No way. Particularly not the dead ones. Luckily, I guess, Jack's mum had already shacked up with some rich transport company boss, the guy who pays for him to come here.

Mrs Foster called the picture 'mesmerising' and hung it in one of the display frames on the Art room corridor; the one next to the window. It looked out of place next to all the other frames with their neat scale drawings and straight lines.

It's lucky that Jack is so amazing at Art. He finds Maths and science properly hard, but if he wins one of the 500 Special Artistic Merit awards he'll only need to get an average of 50 per cent in the other subjects, rather than the normal 70 per cent. Which is actually doable. And Mrs Foster is really helping him prepare his portfolio for the SAMs. She calls Jack her 'protégé' and spends so much time with him that it's almost creepy, but she's like the least creepy person imaginable and definitely not a paedo, so it's all good.

I wish I was someone's protégé. Most teachers, apart from Ms Jones, reasonably like me. But it's often a kind of pitying kind of like. Whenever they say, 'Really well done,' I know in their heads they're also saying, 'for a Norm.' It's like they don't want to invest too much in me as chances are I'll be shipped off to be a Fish. I'll show them!

At the end of the lesson, lots of the freakoids' pieces of paper were still blank. Ha ha. That's what a malcy 0 per cent looks like!

Jack's just given me an amazingly cool picture he's done. He cycled round to mine after dinner, rang the bell and thrust it into my hands. It's of two kids playing by the stream and the water just seems to shimmer on the page. But the best part is that it's of us. Six-year-old us. Six-year-old me clutching a tattered red kite and six-year-old him brandishing a stick.

'Do you remember the day?' Jack asked.

Of course I do. It was my sixth birthday. Mum and Dad had given me a kite for my birthday and Jack and I had raced to People's Park to try it out. I ended up flying it through a bramble bush into a huge patch of nettles and Jack, knowing how much the kite meant to me, charged into the nettles to get it back. He tried to beat a path through them with this big stick. He was just wearing a pair of shorts so his legs were stung raw, but he came out grinning anyway. That's when we jumped into the stream, to cool off. Rex leapt in after us and kept shaking himself, covering us with freezing droplets, and we couldn't stop laughing. Funny to think that you could do that back then. That the streams weren't always infected. It'd be rather less hilarious now.

'I just thought of this. I don't know why. So I painted it. It's a present.'

And that's part of what I love about Jack. He'll do things that other guys would think are tragic or limp, but they're not. They're really cool.

Jack and I have been friends forever. On the surface we couldn't be more different. I've got properly yellow (or as Daisy says 'pus-coloured') curly hair and green eyes. I prefer the term butter-yellow, but Daisy won't believe that I've ever seen, let alone tasted butter, as even when there were still cows it was reserved for the massively super-important. I have though. Tried it, that is. Mum got some years ago in a Ministry hamper and it was so good that I actually licked my plate and knife afterwards, grim, I know! My hair's bound to end up mousy brown, annoyingly, as both Mum and Dad have brown hair and only people who are practically albino stay blonde past their teens anyway. I'll have to dye it, although I'd need to make sure I do a better job than Amanda who dyed hers 'ash blonde' last year but it came out more grey than blonde and she looked like a granny who'd had a face transplant.

Jack, on the other hand, looks like he's descended from a Viking warrior. He's so broad and tall that other schools look at him massively suspiciously when he turns up to sports matches, as if they think we've smuggled in some 17 year old to play against them. He's got carrot-red hair (he'd say strawberry-blond – but it's not) and his face, upper chest and arms are covered in an explosion of orange freckles. He fries if the sun so much as looks at him so maybe he's actually descended from a Viking warrior vampire.

Jack's the kindest, most loyal friend anyone could have. We were born on the same street and have played together from the age of three. He moved to a bigger place when he was seven though – when his mum left his dad for his step-dad. I guess, although you get tonnes of perks and subsidies working for the Ministry like Mum does, if you're just looking at the money side of it, a transport magnate does loads better. Our parents were never exactly great friends. Mum and Dad thought Jack's dad was a bit too 'political' for their taste and that his mum was, I don't know, superficial and a massive pain. I mean, she still spells my name Noah even though Jack's told her about 1000 times there's no 'h'.

They were a real odd couple come to think of it. His dad was into rallies and 'opening people's eyes to the abomination that is the Ministry' while his mum was into facials and boob jobs. I remember Jack being mortified when his mum had her first boob job. We were probably ten at the time and sunbathing in People's Park. His mum took her top off (already cringeworthily embarrassing) and her boobs (covered by tiny triangles of bikini) just sort of defied gravity and stayed shooting up into the air like proud sandcastles. I can't believe you're allowed to dress (or undress) like that in public. I mean, wear a hat and some police guy will pounce as you might be 'unidentifiable on CCTV' for a split millisecond, but make everyone in a park want to puke, no problem!

No one was surprised when she left his dad. Nor I guess when his dad was taken. He was the first person I actually knew who'd been 'eliminated' and it freaked me out for ages. Not for as long as Jack, obviously. He's still not over it. Never will be.

I think I'll hang the picture over my desk. That way I can look at it while I'm revising. Which I guess I'll be doing FOR THE REST OF MY LIFE, or until the fifth of June anyway.

I've just circled the date in red on my calendar.

And breathe…

Just spent the whole weekend at Daisy's. Mum and Dad went away to the Woods for their wedding anniversary. They do it every year. Dad calls it their 'romantic break *à deux*', which he thinks sounds cool as it's got two French words in it. Mum always literally flinches and hisses, '*Ben,*' when he says this. I don't know if it's because it's SO completely cringeworthy or because using French is A-not-OK. They did try to invade us after all. Western France is underwater – let's go and live in Britain. Nice.

Anyway, time with Daisy is always good. We spent the whole day hanging out with Jack by the pond. Jack and I had a competition to see who could skim a stone the furthest and when I won Jack grabbed me and held me upside down so the end of my hair dipped in the water. I yelled at him to pull me out as I didn't want my hair in that disease pool. I mean, if it's got something in it that can kill fish, it can probably make your hair fall out and then I'll never have a boyfriend, ever.

Jack pulled me upright again and held me for a second with my face just centimetres from his. I'm pretty sure he'd had toast for breakfast.

'Kiss already,' Daisy shouted, which was really embarrassing and also completely nicked from *Girl Town*, the most tragic show to have ever been broadcast. TV's pretty awful at the moment, not that Mum hardly lets me watch anyway. Apart from about two OK programmes, there's just endless malc entertainment shows and Bulletins, Bulletins and more Bulletins about our glorious Territory. Maybe it's trying to make us so brain dead that we won't mind when we fail the TAA or maybe it's some cunning plan to send us tunnelling under the fence just to escape the Bulletins. A watery death with a surprising upside.

Daisy won't accept that Jack and I are just friends (best friends, joint with Daisy) and have been since forever. It'd be like kissing my brother, that's if I had one. OK, well, maybe not quite like kissing my brother. Kissing my brother if a little bit of me was into incest.

We used long sticks to look for frogspawn under the giant lily pads past the bridge, but couldn't find any. I didn't mind too much. Last year when we found some and put it in a jar and loads of tiny tadpoles hatched, the tadpoles started eating each other, which was really grim. This year the layer of algae on the pond looks thicker and yellower. There weren't any dead animals floating in it though. That was the first sign with the rivers. Fish everywhere. Floating belly up. With dead eyes, white spots and yellowy gills. It was weird looking at them. Feeling a weird mix of hunger and revulsion.

In the evening we went back to Daisy's. Jack couldn't come as he said he had to help his mum with something, but I think it was also because he knows Daisy's mum doesn't like him. I don't think Daisy's mum really likes me either, but she knows I always do pretty well in tests so I think she hopes I'll help Daisy study more. Be a 'good influence'.

We didn't study though. It was Saturday night after all. Daisy turned on her Scribe and we danced around her room to Kaio. Probably the coolest music the Ministry's ever provided. I know it's seen as slightly malc to be into Kaio big-time, as he's a Ministry pet and everything, but I don't care. He's still amazing, hot beyond hot, and the only way you're going to hear anything better is if you somehow manage to get a massively illegal radio and tune into a massively illegal Opposition-run station. Strangely enough, I don't have any contacts in the secret underground world of illegal radio providers and I don't believe anyone who says they've listened to one really has. I mean Ben in the year below said his cousin had one, but then it changed to his cousin's friend, and when I kept on at him about what the songs were like he looked shifty and sweaty and mumbled something that sounded suspiciously like *Into the Dark* mixed with *Faith*.

Daisy is a REALLY good dancer. She knows how to twist her hips in a really sexy way. If I do it, I look like a complete denser.

At one point she was gyrating against the wall and I wished Jack had been there to see it. Jack gets really embarrassed when Daisy goes all flirty. His cheeks and the bit of chest just below his neck go all red and his freckles seem to leap out at you, almost neon in their orangeness. Like that really orange drink everyone was drinking last year that got banned because it made toddlers turn orange and go hyper. If you tease him about it, he goes even redder. Daisy says he'd go scarlet and probably explode like some giant supernova if I ever properly flirted with him, but she's just trying to stir things up (and show off that she now knows the word 'supernova' after flunking last week's Physics test). Looks-wise (and it seems dance-wise) I'm no Daisy.

Boys like Daisy and Daisy likes it that boys like her. She's kissed eight boys in total and that's excluding kisses without tongues. She can't believe I haven't kissed anyone yet; won't stop teasing me about it. Her two major bits of advice are (1) be careful not to clash teeth as it feels horrible and you look like a right amateur; and (2) make sure the boy hasn't just eaten a piece of cheese on toast like when she kissed Rory Pike and his whole mouth tasted like slightly stale melted cheese, which was grim.

We didn't get to dance for long though. Daisy's stressy mum had a go at us for disturbing Logan. Which is ridiculous as it was only 9pm and what normal twenty year old would care about a bit of music? Particularly amazingly cool music. But I guess Daisy's brother isn't exactly a normal twenty year old. He's a freakoid for a start.

I was really shocked when I first went back to Daisy's at the start of Year 4 and saw that her brother had a Node; was one of them. 'Cos Daisy's not, obviously. Daisy doesn't like to talk about it. Apparently her parents used to be better off. Her dad was the head of some big computer company and so they could afford the procedure – could go make themselves a Childe.

Five years later, things weren't quite so rosy. Another freakoid was out of the question. Daisy always says that she was a mistake. I always tell her she's being a denser, but there is something about the way her mum looks at her sometimes, when she doesn't think anyone else is looking, that is really pretty cold. Kind of scary. Like Mr Hughes with Jack's Physics homework. And she gets so stressed about any test or exam. I guess she's not used to the pressure. Logan naturally sailed through everything. I remember thinking he was quite hot when I first met him, but now I can't see it all. He has Daisy's great cheekbones and perfectly spaced eyes but whereas Daisy gives off this amazing energy, he is a personality black hole. Whenever I see him, I know he's judging me. And by the look on his face, I'm clearly failing.

Once, when Daisy and I were having one of our late-night chats, Daisy asked me whether I thought my parents would come to the Wetlands with me if I failed.

I didn't have to think. 'Yes.' I said. They can be right pains, but Mum and Dad would never let me go by myself. I know they'd do anything to protect me.

Daisy seemed to withdraw into herself a bit. 'Mine would stay,' she said eventually. 'They'd choose Logan.' I tried to reassure her and banged on about it never coming to that anyway, I mean her average test scores are kind of OK at the moment. But I know she's right. There's no way her mum, with her perfectly coiffed hair and diary crammed full of coffee mornings, would pack up and move to a malarial swampland. Not for her child. Well, certainly not for her daughter.

Some evenings can be boring, but this evening was the WORST.

Mum had been invited round to her boss' for dinner and me and Dad had to go too. Which is ridiculous really – surely the only thing that matters is whether Mum is good at her job (which she is) not whether Dad and I can scrub up well and make polite conversation (which we can't – or at least I can't – Dad's better at being phoney polite. He's a lawyer, he has to be.) Anyway, we had to be there for 6pm, which is massively early, so they could have pre-dinner drinks while I hung out with their freakoid son, Charles. And you can tell by the fact that he calls himself Charles, rather than Charlie, what great fun he is.

Their house is in the Western Suburbs, pretty close to the Laboratory and to People's Park. Not that they'd hang out there. They are far too snobby to mix with the common people. Their house is properly massive. A huge black front door that screams 'money' leads into an enormous hallway, with its own fan. And I thought there was supposed to be a lack of space. I know, great idea – let's ship some fifteen-year-old Norms off to die so that the Brooks have enough space for their coats.

I remember talking to Dad about this stuff ages ago. 'Cos nearly everyone we know has a similar sort of apartment. A SMALL similar sort of apartment. Just big enough for a kitchen, separate lounge, and two bedrooms. Enough space for parents and up to two kids. Not that anyone's going to have more than two. If they're Norms you're pretty lucky if one passes. Two pass – you've seriously lucked out. Three – no way. And if you go the freakoid route, well, they're massively expensive to make. Anyway, I'd ranted at Dad about how unfair it was that some people have massive apartments and houses while everyone else is squashed in, and how surely it'd be better to turn the massive apartments and houses into smaller ones so that more people could live in the Territory and more lives could be saved. And then, while we're thinking about it, why not build over all the People's Parks (there must be at least five if each city's got one) and come to think of it, the Woods as well? I guess we'd need to keep the Solar Fields for Energy, but we could probably shrink the Arable Lands a bit more if we just built a few more macro plants or Synthmeat factories. We could let thousands and thousands more people stay, rather than drastically cut the few millions we have.

But Dad said it was all based on research. The neeks decided that we need the Woods to suck up more CO_2 and reduce winter flooding (and so Ministry bigwigs and richer people can go on holiday or for a nice stroll) and we're only just managing to feed the population as it is.

Also, the whole Ministry is based on the idea that in

order for the Territory to survive as sea levels keep going up, the greatest minds have to be motivated to work as hard as possible. To come up with new inventions, new energy resources, new ways of making food. New ways of cooling the planet.

But, I said, pretty densely I guess, surely everyone works really hard to make life better for everyone anyway, don't they?

Dad did a sort of sad smile. Apparently, the good of the Territory isn't concrete enough of a thing to motivate people. The studies showed that people work hardest if (1) they've got space to exercise and relax; and (2) they're going to 'gain materially': get money and stuff. Basically they work hardest if they think that there's a chance they'll get to live in a bigger, better house than everyone else and go on holiday. People don't actually care that much about improving the lives of people they don't know. Equality doesn't work. Humans are rubbish.

Anyway, back to the evening. As soon as we got there, I was ushered into Charles' room. 'Oooooh,' Daisy would say as she so wants me to get a boyfriend, probably even a freakoid. But Charles is seriously not 'Oooooh'; he's 'Urrrgghggh'. Short and stocky with a flat, piggy nose. Charles is in the same year as us at Hollets but in Mr Rice's class. The idea was that we would both do our homework and then chat. As if we'd have anything to talk about. Mum's boss' wife (Jane the Pain) then looked fake-worried and said there was only one Port so we'd have to take it in turns. I said that wouldn't be necessary as I was a Norm and she did a phoney little laugh and said, 'Oh yes, of course, silly me. Good for you,' as if she didn't already know and as if I were some sort of charity case.

'Doing homework' with Charles made me really, really angry. We've got a Geography test tomorrow so had to cram the whole of the stagnant water and malaria topic – four whole weeks' worth of notes. I was there, staring at my Scribe, making flashcards and reading and re-reading while Charles went to his Port.

This was the first time I've really watched someone upload. I mean, there are obviously Ports in the school library, but there are screens in the way, and I don't have any freakoid friends.

Charles switched his Port on. He took the Port's lead, drew it around his neck and quickly plugged it into his Node. He didn't need to even look in the mirror to find the hole, he'd done it so many times.

He pressed the 'upload' icon. There was a pause and then his body went all limp. His eyes rolled upwards and to the right until they looked like white discs and his arms started to twitch. Slowly at first, rhythmically, and then faster until it seemed like he was having some kind of controlled fit. The whole thing only lasted about two minutes and then his eyes returned to normal, his body stiffened and he unplugged.

'Test me on something,' he commanded.

'What percentage of people in the Wetlands die from malaria?' I asked.

'Eighty-four per cent,' he fired back.

I nodded.

'Great – always like to check the upload worked,' he said smugly and then opened up a comic on his Scribe.

Jane the Pain put her head round the door at 7pm to 'see how we were doing'. She congratulated Charles for having finished his homework (yeah right – well done for sitting still and twitching for two minutes) and looked at me with pity again, as if I were some sort of special case denser for still studying.

When I got home I shut myself in the bathroom and used Dad's shaving mirror to look at the back of my neck. There are the bumps of the vertebrae, some downy fair hair and three moles. I can't imagine what it would be like to have two holes there instead. Plugging a lead into your body. Would it be uncomfortable? Would it get hot when the electricity flowed? It just seems so sick. I feel ill if I do something as supposedly harmless as use my fingernail to clean inside my ears. I always visualise it getting stuck or my hand somehow slipping and it accidentally getting rammed into my brain.

One of my moles seems a bit raised. I hope it doesn't grow a hair. Ms Jones has a hairy mole on the left side of her face, just under her ear, and it's reek.

History is just a massive bunch of lies.

It was the twenty-third Anniversary of the Territory today so normal lessons were suspended and we just did History all day.

It kicked off, as it always does, with a ridiculously long assembly. We had to sing the anthem and listen to Mr Daniels droning on about strength in adversity and the birth of our 'Glorious Territory' blah de blah de blah. I'm surprised they didn't make us wave flags or something equally malc.

I can recite the official version off by heart I've heard it so many times. Daisy can too. We once paraded around her bedroom wearing sheets tied round our necks reciting it in loud voices. Thinking back now I'm not sure what the sheets were for. Some kind of superhero cape? 'Territory Man to the Rescue!'

Anyway here it goes:

'After the Great Floods, over half of the world's land mass, including that of Old Britain was under saltwater. The south of Old Britain was submerged and the flooded eastern areas, now known as the Wetlands, became uninhabitable. The soil was saturated with salt so no crops could grow and any remaining freshwater became a breeding ground for disease-carrying mosquitoes. Everyone in Old Britain moved to the central dry land now known as the Territory, but there wasn't enough land to support and feed the existing population. These were the Dark Days. War and famine raged. Then came a new era of peace. The new government, the Ministry, recognised that limited space requires limited numbers. It was imperative for the survival of mankind that the best minds stay in the Territory. Therefore on 1 June 2036 the Fence was built and it was determined that all future children sit a Territorial Allocation Assessment in the summer of their fifteenth year. Those that pass may remain in the Territory, but those that fail will be detained and resettled in the Wetlands. The test is fair as it applies equally to all children regardless of colour, background or creed.'

Then the whole assembly has to join in: 'Limited space requires limited numbers. Difficult situations require difficult decisions.'

I made sure I was sitting next to Jack and Daisy. Us Norms have to stick together on Territory Day, just to make sure none of us reacts. Which is hard. Very hard.

This is what they never say in Assembly:

It's massively unfair that the adults didn't have to sit the TAA. Do you really think they would have voted for it if they had? And now it's too late. 'Cos no one gets to vote anymore. And to start with, the TAA supposedly wasn't that hard. Now, 'cos sea levels are still rising faster than anyone thought, it's massively hard and they're using it to get rid of loads of us. And after the invention of the Childe procedure, how can anyone claim the TAA is fair? I mean only one freakoid has failed in the past three years. Only one! And he was a real-life denser. But thousands of Norms get shipped off every year. And they bang on as if everyone loves (or as Daisy would say *luuuuurrrrrvvves*) the Territory. But then why are there so many police and cameras everywhere? Why did they ban the internet and mobiles for non-Ministry people as soon as they were properly in power? They also keep pretty schtum about the Opposition that Jack's dad belongs to. Sorry *belonged* to. Before they labelled him a Subversive and shot him.

Class-time was next and Ms Jones was out to provoke us. She hates us Norms more than any other teacher in the school. It's because her sister was killed in an Opposition rally that got out of hand. The rally was supposed to be a peaceful protest against the TAA and its bias against Norms, but something went wrong. One hundred and twenty-six people were trampled to death. That's when they banned the Opposition. I know it was a terrible thing to happen and I get why Ms Jones has anger in her, but it's also pretty pathetic that she tries to take it out on us, just because we're easy targets.

The whole class had to sit in a circle. A circle! I mean I haven't sat in a circle since I was five! We had to go round and say something about the Territory that we were grateful for.

'I'll start,' she chirped like some sort of evil bird. 'I'm grateful to the Territory for providing a safe haven for humanity after the Great Flood.'

I clenched Jack's hand to stop myself from reacting.

Freddie, a lame nobody freakoid, went next. 'I'm grateful for the mosquito grids so we don't all get malaria.' Well good for you, Freddie. What about the Fish? Do you think they're grateful too?

But most freakoids just nodded happily. That's the most annoying thing. Most of them know there's no way they're going to fail in June so there's nothing for them to worry about. For them I guess the Territory and TAA are good. Loads of other kids that they don't mix with and won't miss will get moved off the nice dry land so there's more space for them.

Hugo put up his hand and Ms Jones smiled her encouragement. It was as if he'd just read my mind.

'I'm grateful because the Territory ships off all the scummers so they can't leach off us anymore.'

Nearly all the freakoids tittered away, Amanda's attention-seeking giggle drowning out everyone else's. She makes it high and bubbly as she thinks it's sexy, but it's not. It's just massively annoying. But the most annoying thing was that Ms Jones sniggered too before she thought to stop herself.

That's another problem with this place. All the teachers seem to think they're above us Norms. But they're not.

They predate the Procedure. They don't have Nodes. They're Norms through and through. They just think that they'd be freakoids if they were born now. That they're super-beings because they know things (wow – they've been around longer and have the answers in front of them). I bet they'd all have late upgrades if you could do it that late. But you can't. They tried doing ones on adults at the start. All the adults died. Something about the brain still having to be growing in order to accept the wires.

Next thing I knew it was all quiet and I realised that everyone was looking at me. Waiting to hear what I was grateful for.

I tried to think of something nice. 'Think fluffy,' is always Jack's advice. Good advice. I ignored it.

'I'm grateful that the TAA shows that some Norms can do as well as Childes even with a massively unfair disadvantage.'

Ms Jones looked unimpressed but there was little for her to attack. I'd been grateful. And I hadn't said freakoid.

But she couldn't resist being evil.

She turned to Jack and said, 'Jack Munro, we haven't heard from you yet, have we? What are you grateful for?'

I could see Jack struggling. She was smiling. Red lipstick stained her front teeth.

'Are you grateful for our brave police force, chasing down and eliminating Subversives?'

Silence crackled.

Luckily the bell rang at that exact moment so Jack got to leave the room. He punched the wall as we walked to the next lesson. His knuckles bled pretty badly and he left a reddish stain on the paint. I told him to put ice on it as soon as he got home.

Another thing – I didn't point it out to Jack 'cos I didn't want to alarm him, but as we walked down the Art corridor to get to final period, I saw that the frame next to the window had been changed. Jack's charcoal sketch had been removed and a scale drawing of a ruler now sat in its place.

We're going to have a party! Well, when I say 'we' I mean Daisy, but Jack and I are going to help organise it. Daisy's parents are going away in a fortnight and Logan's doing his clinical exam in the Third City as it has THE BEST medical programme, so her house will be completely empty. Logan's going to be a doctor. Great. He'll have one incredible bedside manner.

Daisy's told her parents that she's going to stay at mine and they won't think to check with my parents that it's OK. They're really self-centred like that. Just assume that if they want something to happen because it's convenient for them, then it will.

Daisy, Jack and I met by the benches at the east corner of People's Park to start planning. It was a hot day so we wanted to be outside. I think we were all relieved to have something to focus on after Territory Day. It might seem a bit weird throwing a party with the TAA just weeks away (ten weeks one day – not that I'm counting!) but I think people kind of need it. Freakoids, not that we'll probably be inviting many, can go out all they want as they're pretty certain they'll pass so the TAA isn't such a big deal for them. Us Norms know that we might well only have very limited time left here so, as well as revising our guts out, we need to cherish life as we know it now, before … well, you know before what.

'Who shall we invite?' Daisy asked, pen poised over a notebook she'd covered in malc doodles of flowers.

'Please tell me you haven't started a new book for the party?' I said, rolling my eyes. Daisy likes 'pretty things' (think pretty tacky) and has to start some new flowery/generally grim notebook every time she begins a new project. If she put as much time into making flashcards she could sell them for massive amounts to younger students, and probably actually remember some stuff.

As we started going through who we wanted to invite/would rather be thrown off a bridge than spend time with, a strange figure stumbled out of the bushes towards us. A boy, probably twelve or thirteen, with a shock of curly brown hair. His arms hung limply by his side and he walked with a weird, lurching gait. His eyes looked at us, but seemed blank, as if he wasn't registering what he was seeing, and a thin spittle of saliva hung off his bottom lip like the beginnings of a spider's web.

I had a sudden, sick realisation.

Daisy must have seen my face because she turned to me and whispered, 'Who's that?'

'That's Jimmy White.' I whispered back and we both shrank into the bench a little. Everyone in our area knew the name. He had been a year below us at Hollets and had been a slightly below-average student. He was born a Norm as his parents hadn't been rich enough to afford the procedure to make a Childe. Anyway, when Jimmy turned eleven, his dad unexpectedly made partner at the big accountancy firm he'd worked at forever. With the promotion came a fat bonus. His dad spent it all on a late upgrade for his son.

Everyone knows the procedure has its risks. The surgeons have to cut between your second and third vertebrae to imbed the Node and wire and then drill through your skull to insert a chip into the important memory bit of your brain. It has a Latin name. I don't know Latin. A miniscule error – a shake of the hand, the wrong-sized scalpel – can mean any number of massively important neurones are cut and hey presto, you're a vegetable.

You can see why some parents still do it though. Mistakes are really rare and successful late upgrades are just as likely as full-on Childes to pass the TAA. There's a bit of a stigma attached to it and they'll always be slight outsiders, but if you're a Mum or Dad weighing that up against losing your child to near certain death as a Fish, you probably don't care too much about the odd snobby look or withheld birthday invite.

Unfortunately for Jimmy, the surgeon's hand shook. He'll now spend the next year and a bit wandering round aimlessly until he fails the TAA and is shipped off. I don't know if they'll even make him sit it. Or, if he's judged enough of a vegetable, his parents will have the right to sell him for organ transplants. Want a new conservatory? Just sell Jimmy's kidneys. Nice.

Luckily, a late upgrade isn't much of a risk for Jack, Daisy or me. My parents could have had a Childe pretty cheaply if they'd wanted to – it's another Ministry perk for top scientists. But they were both against it on principle. They just didn't like the idea of someone else being able to put information in my head.

'If they can upload information, it's only a matter of time before they can upload thoughts or emotions,' Dad says. He can be slightly paranoid. Maybe they'd have thought differently if I hadn't found school easy. I don't know.

Jack's step-dad is only paying the massively high

Hollets fees to please Jack's mum. He's not exactly going to shell out even more for someone else's kid. I mean, I'm sure he cares about Jack and everything, but his life would actually be easier if Jack was shipped off in June and he had Jack's mum and her inappropriate low-cut tops and droopy cleavage all to himself.

As for Daisy, her parents probably would pay for it if they could afford it. But they can't. So Daisy's safe from that at least. She just needs to work harder. A lot harder.

We abandoned party planning after Jimmy. Decided we'd invite the people already on our list and take it from there. I mean I'll probably just talk to Daisy and Jack the whole night anyway.

Genes are strange things. Amanda is about as horrific a person as you can get, but her mum's actually really nice.

I bumped into her this evening, forehead smack literally, on the way to the refuse centre. Mum and Dad believe in sharing responsibility (or getting out of boring chores by dumping loads on me). I had all our different bags and was already pushing it to get there before the centre shut for the night. I was in a foul mood. One of our bags had burst when I bumped it down the steps at the front of our apartment building. Luckily Mr Patel was just getting home at that exact moment and he dashed in to his apartment and gave me a spare bag. Mr Patel's really nice. I guess Sunaina is just a bit younger than me and a Norm too, so he probably feels a bit protective of me.

Just when I thought my hassles were over, I was stopped by a policewoman at the corner. Officer Brown ('call-me-Marcus'), who's actually alright, must have been off-duty. The policewoman made me go through the different bags to check I wasn't 'concealing anything subversive'. My right hand now stinks of rotting potato peel and boiled mucor and the worst thing is I don't think she even thought I looked remotely suspicious. I think she's just a power hungry witch who likes to make people stick their hands into their own garbage. I'm sure she wouldn't have stopped me if I'd been in my Hollets' uniform.

Anyway, I was stomping along, fed up and bursting with cutting comments I'd like to use to take that police witch down but knew I'd never be allowed to, when I heard the droning in the sky. I looked up. Two plumes of white smoke trailed behind a silver plane, cutting lines into the blue. I think everyone in the street stopped to stare. It was almost beautiful, but also seemed massively unnatural. I know, let's get in a big steel contraption and chuck it up into the sky and hope it stays up. No thanks! Guess it can't be that dangerous if the First Minister uses it. I think the last Bulletin said he was off to the States. No doubt to have his photo taken as they shoot the next batch of mirrors into space. They'll definitely work this time! Yeah right.

Amanda's mum must have been walking the other way and staring up too; it was when the noise faded, we collided. She gave me a hug then wrinkled her nose at the smell, and then tried to pretend she hadn't. She offered to give me some of Amanda's old clothes, even though I'm about 10cm taller than her so there's no way they'd fit. I think she thinks I must be really poor as I'm a Norm. Now she's going to think I have terrible personal hygiene too. I can just imagine her at her next dinner party. 'Do you know poor people smell like rotting potatoes?'

Freakoids aren't always that easy to spot.

A new boy joined our class today: Raf Ferris. Ms Jones introduced him at registration. No one paid much attention at first. He seemed unremarkable. He was wearing scuffed blue jeans and a brown jumper with a small hole at the elbow. And a scarf. Even though it really wasn't that cold. Jack thought he looked like a right poser. It was only when Raf looked up that everyone took notice. He has these really weird, intense eyes. The left one is bright green but the right one is bright blue. I never even knew a person could have eyes like that. I remember a neighbourhood cat when I was really small having one yellow and one green eye, but never a person.

Hugo sniggered and then obviously Amanda, his lame shadow, started laughing too. They are so predictable. Laughing at anything that is not compleeeeetley perfect. I think his eyes are cool though. Better than perfect. When the freakoids started laughing, Raf just grinned and kept chewing the gum in his mouth. He has a really cool grin. I must have been grinning too 'cos Daisy poked me in the ribs and whispered in my ear, 'You so luuurrrvve him'. Which I so don't, obviously. I don't even know him.

Ms Jones told Raf to go and sit down and then told him to take off his scarf as it wasn't 'suitable attire' for the classroom. She also told him that he needed to buy or borrow a school uniform by tomorrow morning.

'I am not sure how they ran things at your last school, Rafael, but we do things properly at Hollets. A smart appearance is one step closer to a smart mind.'

She is such a pain, Ms Jones. She says so many completely annoying things that I think she must have a book of annoying phrases somewhere at home and selects a new one every morning.

'And dispose of your chewing gum this instant. We do not chew the cud. We are not cattle.'

Some days it seems she selects two. And great joke, as there aren't any cows anymore, except her of course.

When Raf unwrapped his scarf I gasped. There, at the

back of his neck, between the second and third vertebrae, was a Node – clear as anything. I prodded Daisy in the ribs and her mouth literally fell open too. At the same time I saw Hugo and Quentin just stop and stare and even Ms Jones flinched. I don't know who was more shocked: me and Daisy to find out that the cool new boy was actually a freakoid Childe or the freakoids to find out that the mutant-eyed messy boy was actually one of them.

I really don't get sport. We have to do loads of it, even with the TAA looming, as some Ministry idiot seems to think it'll help the formation of some new strong, healthy, intelligent master race that'll lead us out of our current problems. There's even an exceptionally lame poster in the changing rooms showing a group of guys, supposedly fifteen but even more built than Jack, with the slogan, 'Team building builds the Territory'. I mean, what crap! As if these teen sporting heroes are going to use their over-developed biceps to somehow pump the Wetlands dry, Superman-style. Methinks not. More likely they're going to be moaning about torn hamstrings and knee injuries while sitting at their boring desk jobs or dying in the Wetlands as one too many tackle knocked out one too many brain cell.

All lessons were cancelled this afternoon so the whole school could watch our Rugby First Team play in the Schools' Final against Higgins High, our main rival. Everyone was absurdly excited about the game. Loads of students were wearing or waving the Hollets scarf (super lame and super grim tan and black stripes) and Amanda and some other freakoid girls had painted glittery 'H's on their cheeks, lost in the ecstasy of getting to watch Hugo and Quentin run around in short shorts.

Daisy whispered in my ear, 'Do you think we should tell them Higgins High also starts with an H?' and I cracked up. Amanda glared at us, not knowing what the joke was, but knowing it was at her expense.

Normally Daisy and I would have skived something like this at all costs, but this time Jack was playing and, knowing this was pretty important to him, we thought we really should support him. He'd been included last minute as Felix, the normal winger, had hurt his shoulder. So when the bell rang, we dutifully filed onto the spectator benches with everyone else and began edging along the row to an empty space. I was looking at the pitch rather than where I was going, so I didn't stop when the guy in front of me did and ended up embarrassingly tumbling into his lap like a full-on denser. I heard a bump as something fell to the ground.

Looking up, blushing furiously, I saw that I'd landed on Raf, the new freakoid. I stood up, cringing and expecting him to have a massive go at me, trashing me and Norms in general in the usual freakoid way. Fish, Fish, Fish.

Instead, he flashed me an incredible grin and I got to see those magical eyes close up.

'Um, sorry about that,' I mumbled. Possibly not my greatest verbal effort, but it was the best I could manage as I stood and straightened myself up. And then I remembered the 'bump'. 'Oh God, I think I knocked something onto the ground. I hope it's not broken.'

'No problem, really. Please don't worry,' Raf insisted a little too much. Like an idiot, I ignored him and dived down again (realising when on the ground that I was far too close to his crotch) returning with a battered paperback book.

'Thanks,' Raf said quietly, and tucked the book into his coat pocket before too many prying eyes took notice. Reading's pretty unusual and reading actual books, rather than the official books supplied on your Scribe, is seen as BAD. Dad only lets me read the books he gives me at home. I guess different rules apply to freakoids. The chances of them growing up and joining the Opposition are a big fat zero so they don't have the same police attention.

I'd seen the title: *Great Expectations*.

'It's good. The book, I mean,' I said, wanting for some reason to continue the conversation.

Surprise registered on his face. 'You've read it? I thought no one else read this stuff anymore. Yeah, it's brilliant, so far,' Raf replied. 'Thought I might get some reading done while everyone was watching the match.' He gestured at the field and the crowd. 'This isn't really my thing.' Pause. 'I'm Raf by the way.'

His breath smelt of spearmint gum. 'I'm Noa.'

And then the whistle blew and the talking stopped.

I know basically nothing about rugby. Jack's tried to teach me the fundamentals but my brain just switches off. Even so, I could tell that Jack was on fire this afternoon. He seemed to be everywhere at once and moved massively fast for someone so big. Whenever some guy from Higgins had the ball and starting sprinting towards their white line, Jack was there and tackled them down. Huge cheers rang out round the pitch and even freakoids joined in the cheers of, 'Jack, Jack, Jack.' Hugo and Quentin and the others were probably all playing fine, but no one cared. This was Jack's match, and they knew it. I could see the anger on Hugo and Quentin's faces, even though from where I was sitting they were not much more than fork-sized.

Just before the end of the match, it really kicked off. Jack was tripped. And I don't mean tackled. I'm talking deliberately tripped, mid-sprint, by a member of his own team: Quentin. Jack literally somersaulted mid-air and came down with a crunch. Daisy and I were left gasping and pointing and there was a general rumble of concern along the Hollets benches. Even Raf got that something was wrong and looked up from his book in confusion. The referee looked a bit shocked, but there really wasn't anything he could do. It's not like it was a normal team on team foul or anything. I couldn't take my eyes of Jack, willing him to get to his feet, hoping that he and, most importantly, his hands, weren't badly injured.

He eventually got up, winced slightly as he flexed various muscles, and then he slowly and determinedly walked over to Quentin. There was a fixed look on his face and his fists were clenched. I don't know what would have happened next if the end-of-match whistle hadn't blown and the Hollets coach hadn't dragged Jack away and back to the lockers.

Hollets had won and Jack got 'Best Player'.

But victory seemed pretty empty.

I never thought I could actually enjoy an Assembly, but today's was something else. First-class Ace-McSpace. Mr Daniels has had a hair transplant. Yes, I'm talking about a full-on removal of the grey squirrel's tail and all over plugs of golden brown. I think the rumours about him and Ms Forester must be true. She's at least fifteen years' younger than him so this must be his attempt to look thirties rather than fifties. But what a result! He looks RIDICULOUS!

We're calling him Aslan from now on, even Daisy, who wouldn't read anything if she could get away with it and is normally allergic to book references.

We were all made to read *The Lion, the Witch and the Wardrobe* in Year 6. Maybe the Ministry thought that books about 'plucky' kids fending for themselves would somehow make the idea of being shipped off to the Wetlands less terrifying. Yeah right. Shame there's no magic door to escape back through.

Anyway, Mr Daniels has got balls though. He walked up onto the stage and began droning on about God's Love (yeah – not sure his God loves Norms very much) as if nothing whatsoever had happened to his scalp. And then halfway through his limp speech, he actually shook his neck a little to make his hair waft out, like he was a hot sixteen-year-old girl. Jack, Daisy and my shoulders all began to shake like washing machines. I couldn't look at their faces as I knew the laughter would explode out and TAA points would be haemorrhaged. As it was, Mr Daniels seemed to be able to detect the silent shaking as he stopped, mid-sentence, and did search-beam eyes over the Assembly floor.

I stopped breathing as his eyes swept over the three of us. 'Please, please, please don't notice us,' I said in silent prayer to the God I'm not sure I even believe in.

Miraculously, his eyes kept moving and the next thing I knew, some other poor kid was being yelled at.

'You. Yes you there. Stand up. What's your name?'

'Raf.'

I couldn't believe it. The new freakoid boy. He must have been laughing too.

'Raaaaffff.' Mr Daniels drew out his name like he was stretching a rubber band between his teeth. 'You're clearly finding something very amusing. Is there a joke you'd like to share with us?'

'No, sir. Sorry, sir.'

'See me in my office after Assembly.'

'Yes, sir.'

Raf bent his head as he sat down again. He looked a bit scared, but he didn't look properly sorry. He looked like someone acting sorry who's a bit of a bad actor. I hope he doesn't get into too much trouble though. He seems pretty cool for a freakoid. And I swear he was still chewing gum, which is almost a criminal offence at Hollets.

Oh, and Jack got Fished again today. This time it was his locker, which I guess is at least better than his desk. He went to open it at lunch to get out his kit for rugby practice and a super-large, super-grim brown trout plopped out onto the floor. Slime trail down Jack's clothes, dead eye staring back up. A note 'Hello Fish Face' was tied round its neck.

You'd have thought that basically winning the big match single-handedly for Hollets would be seen as a good thing, but the rumour is that someone's going to be bumped from the first team to make a permanent position for Jack, and the freakoids aren't happy about it.

Jack said it didn't bother him. That it just shows what losers the freakoid jocks are. And how much time they have on their hands. Free this weekend? Yes, but after I've walked to the river and put on some rubber gloves and fished out some dead diseased fish.

But no one wants their locker to stink of dead fish. And no one wants to be constantly reminded of what's going to happen if it all goes wrong in June.

I randomly bumped into Raf as I left school. We were walking out down the corridor at the exact same time, at the exact same speed, so we kind of had to talk. I asked him about Mr Daniels and said I hoped he hadn't got into too much trouble. I don't know why, but as soon as I started speaking I could feel this malc blush rise up my face.

Raf clearly noticed as a grin spread over his face and his eyes sort of narrowed at the corners so they looked sly but pretty damn sexy at the same time.

'I got let off with a warning. First time offender.' Raf smiled. 'God he's horrific though. A real idiot. And what does he expect if he does that to his hair anyway?'

I couldn't believe a freakoid would speak that way about a teacher, let alone a headmaster.

Raf misinterpreted my shocked face. 'Sorry if you like him and everything.'

'Oh God no,' I said, and then an image of Mr Daniels

with his hair wafting came back to me and I started giggling. 'We're calling him Aslan now.'

'Aslan, I like it.' His eyes narrowed further to blue/green slits.

And then we were at the exit and I saw Daisy and Jack calling me over and so I had to go as there was no proper reason to stay. And it took everything in me not to look back as I did.

I might be imagining it, but I think Raf might actually like me a bit. You know when you catch someone looking at you and then they look away but it's intentionally a fraction of a second too late so they know you're going to notice them looking anyway.

I first noticed it in double Chemistry. I was sitting at the window end of the front bench. I wasn't being lamely keen; I'm a middle-bench girl by choice but my right contact lens had fallen out in morning break so I couldn't see the board otherwise. Even then I had to squint like a bit of a denser to see the writing clearly. I guess I could have worn my glasses but there was more chance of Hugo declaring undying love for me than that happening. Mum says I look really nice and sophisticated in my glasses and that they're 'fashion glasses', but I know that's code for right geek and 'fashion' means even lamer than normal. I'm pleased she has principles and everything and didn't make me a freakoid, but she could at least have let them laser my eyes. I'm probably the only person at Hollets who even owns a pair of glasses.

Anyway, Raf was sitting in the middle of the front bench, which was surprising. Most freakoids sit at the back as they don't have to concentrate as hard 'cos they're going to upload all the key points later anyway. And there were some spaces free at the back. One next to Amanda, which, OK, even most freakoids would avoid if they didn't fancy a plague of flirtation and coma-inducing giggling. But there was also one next to Barnaby, who's pretty harmless.

To look at the board or watch Mr Malovich, Raf just needed to look straight ahead. But he kept looking left towards the window. And smiling. And it seemed that he was looking at me. I checked and there wasn't anything remotely amusing happening outside. And I wasn't sitting next to someone properly hot like Daisy, as Daisy's in a different Chemistry class. Obviously, it might be that he was laughing at my squinting face, which admittedly is pretty funny in a massively unattractive way. (Daisy says it's not as bad as I think it is but I've done it in front of the mirror and it's pretty hideous.)

But the thing is even that wouldn't be normal freakoid behaviour. Freakoids ridicule Norms all the time. But not normally by smiling. It's usually more direct. 'Hey, Fish Face,' is a classic. Or 'How are the swimming lessons going?' is another piece of hilarity. Fish and Fish Face have now completely taken over as insult of choice. A couple of months ago, Water Monkey was all the rage and it'd be rare for a Norm to walk down the corridor without being treated to a freakoid doing monkey arms and saying, 'Ooo ooo ooo,' interspersed with the odd, 'Glug glug glug'. And who do you think looked more like a denser?

I told Daisy about Raf maybe liking me at lunch and she said she'd check it out in Maths, which we all had together in final period.

'He's definitely looking at you,' she confirmed. 'And he's really cute. For a freakoid.'

'Who is?' Jack had crept up on us without our noticing. Which makes us pretty deaf as he's not exactly a ginger ninja.

Both of us paused, knowing Jack's reaction.

'Raf, the new boy.' Daisy finally replied.

'The new freakoid you mean?' Jack exploded. 'I can't believe you sometimes, Daisy. Get a grip on your hormones, for God's sake. He's a freakoid. End of story. Just one more robotic loser guaranteed to take a Norm's place. Just stay away from him.'

'It's not me he's into.' Daisy spat back.

And then Jack shot me this look. And it was so full of confusion and disappointment that I felt a little bit sick.

So Jack's off the rugby team. Coach Potter told him yesterday evening. From hero to zero in 60 seconds. Apparently the Governors had decided that, in light of the 'incident' last Friday, Jack's being on the team was 'weakening team spirit'.

'I'm sorry, Jack, but it's out of my hands now,' Coach Potter had said.

It's so unfair. Just because some freakoids couldn't handle the fact that a Norm was actually loads better than them and showed them up. And surely if it was the 'incident' that worried them, then it was Quentin, not Jack, who should go. Jack thinks it all came from Quentin's father who's a school Governor. Quentin was one of the weakest on the team so most likely to get bumped if Jack had a permanent place. Quentin's dad also 'sponsors' the team, which basically means that he buys all the uniforms and pays for the minibus to take them to games. He's not exactly going to keep paying for other people's children to be driven round everywhere, while his son sits on the bench like a loser.

At least this should mean Jack stops getting Fished as much and has more time for his SAM project.

I tried to convince him that it was probably all for the best, but although he nodded along and made all the right noises, he still didn't look convinced. I've promised to help him revise for the next three big science tests, as he needs a bit of a boost at the moment. He's also talked me into modelling for his next drawing for his SAM portfolio. That, I am not looking forward to.

Raf sat at our table at lunch today.

We'd been paired together for Chemistry. We were learning about Group 1 metals and both laughed at exactly the same time when Mr Malovich said 'effervesce' in a weirdly squeaky, high voice and then tried to cover it up with a cough. Jack started laughing too, but then stopped when he saw that Raf was laughing. He can be such an idiot sometimes.

Then in the canteen I saw Raf hovering, tableless, with a tray and he caught my eye and walked over.

'Can I join you?' he asked, his incredible eyes looking all, well, incredible. Daisy started smirking in a really annoying way and Jack looked pissed off, but we couldn't just leave him standing there, could we? I think Jack just wouldn't like any freakoid on principle.

Daisy whispered in my ear, 'In there [big pause – the pause is crucial] like swimwear.' I nudged her to shut up, but couldn't stop myself from laughing. It's one of our phrases at the moment. We know it's lame but I guess we find it funny as swimming is out big time. Water's kind of lost its appeal.

Lunch was particularly bland. Mucor loaf with potatoes. We're getting less and less meat (if you can call Synthmeat meat) at the moment and more and more mucor, which only Daisy is happy about as she's become a lame vegetarian. I think it's just to annoy her mum. (It's not going to be for animal cruelty reasons as I don't think tissue cells grown in a factory lab exactly feel pain.) I once actually passed a mucor factory when driving somewhere with Mum. It was really weird: a dozen huge metal cylinder vat things where they grow the fungus and then a more normal-looking factory building where I guess they process it and add all the zillion different flavour combos that always end up tasting pretty much the same anyway, ie grim.

I asked Raf how come he'd moved to Hollets just six weeks before the TAA. As soon as the words were out of my mouth I wanted to claw back my massively boring question. About equal to Daisy's dad asking her first boyfriend if he played a musical instrument. She was mortified. Anyway, Raf's dad had moved jobs – he was a scientist like Mum and had been promoted to head up a team at the Laboratory.

'Robotics?' Daisy butted in. I felt annoyed with her for talking to him, but I guess it wasn't exactly going to be an exclusive conversation, with two other people on the table and everything. And, to be fair to Daisy, everyone wanted to know more about the robots. We've all heard that they're going to make robots to run stuff like the refuse centres and Dad had just been saying the other night how old all the bin men and cleaners and road sweepers were starting to look. I mean Al, who's normally at the refuse centre when I go, looks even weaker than me and I always feel properly guilty when he helps me throw the bags into the different skips. And it's not as if anyone who's had to pass the TAA is going to accept that sort of job. Well done, you've revised your guts out or have incredibly rich parents who've paid to freakoid you up. Now here's a broom.

Raf said that his dad was actually involved in disease-control, like Mum, but even so I could see that all talk was about to turn to robot stuff. It was like I could see my chance to find out more about HIM just start to fade away and I so wanted to talk to him that I did something incredibly embarrassing. I opened my mouth, made a sort of weird gargling 'agh' sound, and then shut it again and flushed fuchsia. Floor swallow me now.

Raf smiled his killer smile again and said, 'Sorry? Is there something you wanted to say?'

Before I had the chance to respond, Hugo barged past and knocked his tray into Raf's back, definitely on purpose.

There was this massively tense pause as everyone waited to see how Raf would react, but Raf just looked up and smiled at Hugo. Not his normal smile. No glinting as it didn't reach his eyes. But his lips were definitely turned up at the corners. I would have decked Hugo. Well, tried to anyway.

'You don't deserve to be a Childe,' Hugo spat at him. 'You're a mutant. Your parents should have disposed of you once they saw you and your disgusting eyes growing in the WombPod.'

Raf just kept on smiling (ish) and started to eat his dessert. This alone was pretty impressive as it was parsnip and honey puree, which everyone knows is grim.

I told Hugo to get lost. I shouldn't have got involved.

'Getting cosy with the new boy are you, Noa? Finally think you're in with a chance of some Childe-action? No one else would touch you. Well, Jack obviously, but he doesn't count, now does he?'

Jack jumped to his feet. I've never seen him so angry. It took all my strength to yank him back down. The last thing he needs now is to be caught fighting in the canteen and have a point deducted.

When Hugo left, I asked Raf how he managed to stay so calm. He said he was just used to it. He'd had it all his life. Freakoids didn't like him and neither did Norms.

'Can't imagine why,' Jack mumbled under his breath. He can be really rude sometimes.

Then Raf leaned in towards me, all mock serious and

minty-fresh breath, and thanked me for 'my concern'. And then he winked. Green and blue to just green and then green and blue again. It was ACE.

Studying with Jack can be quite hard work. It's not that he's stupid, far from it, it's just that our brains work so completely differently. I don't know exactly how I remember stuff. I just seem to read things a lot, make a few flashcards and then it's there in my head. With Jack it's all visual though. If he can picture the thing or link whatever we've got to learn to an image, then he's fine. If not, he's in BIG TROUBLE.

We were revising Chemistry for tomorrow's test. Jack got all the tests for the different elements stuff, as they normally involved some colour change, but then we did equilibria and he was just so lost. I even tried an explanation based on saunas and plunge pools, but his expression turned even blanker. At one point, he got so frustrated he punched the wall again. No major damage this time, just a bit of blood on his knuckles and a slight dent to the right of the light switch. Jack's step-dad must have heard as he yelled up at Jack to, 'Cool it!' which was embarrassingly try-hard. Jack's step-dad thinks he's 'down with the kids'. He's not. He also thinks Jack's got anger issues. Which he does.

Normally Jack's the nicest, kindest guy you could ever imagine, but when he gets massively annoyed or frustrated about something, he goes into caveman mode and punches something. Luckily so far it's always been a wall. He's got a poster above his bed of Florrie Fox and I know he's not really that into her, even though she's really hot, it's just that the poster is the perfect size to cover a hole he punched in the wall there three months ago. It was plasterboard, but I still can't believe his whole hand actually went through! It'd be impressive if it wasn't so dense.

That happened after Jack overheard his step-dad try to convince his mum to send him to a therapist to deal with his issues. 'After all it's not my genes he's inherited. You don't want another Subversive in the family.' Anyone slagging off Jack's dad is like someone pressing a trigger button in Jack's brain. The swelling on his hand took two weeks to go down and he could barely grip a paintbrush all that time.

At least tonight Jack looked really sheepish as soon as he'd punched the wall.

'I just can't do this,' he said. 'And it's all malc anyway. I mean, why do I need to know about some guy called Le Chatelier and how best to make ammonia, but I hardly need to read any books anymore? Do we really want to live somewhere filled with ammonia-making scientists where no one can write a poem?'

I know what he means. They took poetry off the syllabus last year – no one could believe it. You can still do it if you're going for a SAM in Literature but no one at Hollets is being put forward for one. And the few novels we study are SO limp. All about sacrifice and the importance of government.

Dad couldn't believe it when he saw the reading list. He's drawn up his own list of 'classics' for me, from books he's got stashed away in the chest by the sofa.

'At least you've still got Art,' I said.

Jack nodded, nursing his now swelling hand.

'So give your hand a break, OK? No more punching, not until after the exams anyway.'

Jack's given me a sneak preview of his SAM portfolio and it properly rocks. The theme is evolution and he's done charcoal drawings of different species morphing into each other: a bat into a crow, an ant into a rat. They're dark and menacing but beautiful at the same time.

Each year they publish a list of the 500 students who've been awarded a SAM alongside the normal pass/fail lists. So far no one from Hollets has got one. But that's all going to change this year. Jack's going to get one – I know it.

The only other people I know, or rather know of, as I obviously don't know them personally – I wish! – who got a SAM are Kaio and Frankie Lebore. Kaio's like the poster boy for SAMs as they were introduced in his exam year and everyone, even lots of freakoids, thinks his music is

ACE. I mean you have to be pretty cool to be so famous that you don't even need a surname. Kaio always says he was a pretty average student but he could play about twelve instruments by the time he was ten. Whenever anyone criticises the TAA syllabus and its focus on science and facts, Kaio gets wheeled out and the Minister for Education does a big spiel about how SAMs protect creativity so it's all OK. Hmmm.

Frankie Lebore's a super-hot writer and poet and got his SAM two years later. He used to be paraded around too by the Ministry to recite some 'uplifting' poem or short story. But then one year his poem wasn't exactly uplifting – it was supposedly about bullfrogs but everyone knew it was about the fat, corrupt officials at the top of the Ministry, so he's been dropped. The programme was actually pulled from the air halfway through his poem. The look on the news anchor's face was hilarious!

I really didn't feel like going to school today. I had a really malc headache, one that felt like I had a stone lodged behind my left eye. Mum wouldn't let me stay at home though. She said I didn't have a temperature so even if we miraculously got a doctor's appointment, they'd still probably not give me an Approved Absence Certificate and she didn't want to risk losing our food rations for the week. Fair enough, I guess.

My headache seemed to be cured by our Physics test results. I got 85 per cent, which was really cool as I was up there with the freakoids. Jack got 71 per cent, which was a miracle. I mean, 71 per cent in PHYSICS! If he does that in June he'll be safe – and dry! He reached over and dug a pen in my ribs so I'd turn round and he mouthed, 'Thank you!' I gave a mock bow back and then we just grinned stupidly at each other for a while. Daisy got 53 per cent and started fiddling furiously with her hair, which is never a good sign and showed that she was properly upset. I tried to smile at her but she wouldn't look up from her desk. I wish she'd revise more with me and Jack. I think it'd really help her focus, but she says that's not the way she works and she's massively stubborn so she's not about to change her mind now.

The only other result I registered was Raf's. He got 82 per cent, which is obviously good, but not great for a freakoid. I mean, most of the test was just recall so he must have bombed on any 'apply your knowledge' question.

I felt a bit disappointed, to be honest. In my head Raf had become a sort of mini-God: super hot and super clever. But maybe he's just a super-hot, pretty averagely intelligent, less-freakoidy-than-normal freakoid.

But then I walked out of the Physics lab at the same time as him and we did this awkward little dance on the spot as we each tried to let the other one go first. His arm brushed mine and he gave me one of his megawatt smiles and an incredible wink and I thought that maybe being super clever isn't that important after all.

The rest of the day went by in a bit of a blur. Daisy grabbed me and Jack in lunch break, wanting to finalise details for the party. This is Daisy's method of coping, I guess. To manically channel energy into something else.

'So that's everything apart from drink taken care of,' Daisy pronounced.

Jack and I looked at each other doubtfully. Two years ago the Ministry had lowered the age for buying alcohol to fourteen, I guess to let us get drunk in our probable final year on dry land to console ourselves about the rubbish future that loomed for us. You wouldn't see that many freakoids buying it – their world didn't need escaping from in the same way. Loads of parties now involved Norm kids getting massively wasted and puking everywhere. This wasn't quite what I'd had in mind. Also the one time I got drunk, at Jack's last birthday, I had a terrible hangover and I can't exactly afford to lose any study days at the moment.

Daisy never really thinks about consequences or the future or anything like that, so she was up for buying loads of booze. Luckily however, Jack agreed with me, so Daisy was overruled and stormed off in a bit of a huff. She can be pretty melodramatic sometimes.

Right and wrong should be simple but it's not.

Instead of Assembly this morning, we all had to sit in the Hall and watch the latest Bulletin. Clearly something big had happened. We were all expecting news of some great triumph like the new mirrors already reducing global temperatures by 0.0001 degrees or some scientist (Ministry sponsored of course) finding a way to refreeze the poles. We weren't expecting the images we saw. Mr Daniels informed us that we might find the Bulletin 'distressing'.

'Not as distressing as your hair,' Daisy mumbled, which had Jack and me shaking, and then we took it to the next level with an unstoppable mini Mexican wave of eyebrow raising.

'Shhhh,' came the command from the front and we froze before we could be identified.

The screen flickered to life. The familiar countdown 3 – 2 – 1 and then Daniel Steven appeared, the supposedly friendly face of the Ministry. He's awful and clearly has no friends. This morning he was playing serious. You could tell by the calculated furrow in his forehead and the way he had adjusted his eyes to a 'concerned but determined' expression.

'Fellow citizens of the Territory,' he began. What a

faker. 'In the early hours of this morning, a heinous act was committed. A bomb was detonated at a WombPod Facility in the Third City destroying ninety-three Childe foetuses and killing three technicians.' Images of a blown-up building appeared on the screen followed by image after image of fragmented Wombpod, the floor a carpet of blood. Bile rose in my throat and little gasping cries went up throughout the hall. All I could think was, they killed all those babies. I can't believe they actually killed all those babies. Someone fainted at the back of the room and another teacher ran out, the door slamming behind her. 'The attack was orchestrated by the Opposition. The perpetrators have all been apprehended by our tireless police force and are now in custody awaiting trial.' Images of about ten men and three women were paraded across the screen. They were all quite old. Their faces were dirty. Most had black eyes or cuts to their faces. One had a weird nervous tic. I felt this hatred rise up in me and I wanted to hurt them too. Erase them to erase what they'd done. I didn't know I had these feelings in me. I mean, I hate Mr Daniels and most of the teachers at Hollets. Oh, and Hugo and Quentin while I'm at it, but this hatred felt deeper. More instinctive. And it was accompanied with a real desire to inflict pain.

The Bulletin was over and Mr Daniels dismissed us.

Everyone started talking immediately and for once the teachers let us. The conclusion bubbling round the hall was that the Opposition deserved to die. All of them. Every Opposition member deserved to die.

Someone tripped over my feet and it was only then that I realised that I was still sitting on the floor, so lost in my thoughts that I'd forgotten to even stand up. I'd always admired the Opposition. Never planned to join them, I like being alive too much for that, but I'd admired their courage, their conviction. Jack, next to me, had his head in his hands. Someone spat on him as they walked past.

He looked up at me, his eyes confused and sad.

The rest of the day seemed to drag on and on and I was exhausted by the time I got home.

Dad got back from work before Mum. He saw me curled up on the sofa and came and gave me a big hug. I told him about the Bulletin and he got so angry. At first I thought he was angry at me, but it soon became clear that he was mad at the school, for showing the Bulletin that is. 'Completely inappropriate,' he kept saying. 'Could give kids nightmares.' I kept protesting that I'm not actually a kid anymore, but it's like Dad's got weird eyes that distort all images of me into those of a ten-year-old girl.

'But how could they do that?' I asked. 'How could they think it was OK to kill all those babies?' That was the one question I couldn't get out of my head. Dad looked around and then started to whisper. I think it was just a reflex reaction as no one thinks they're actually bugging flats yet.

'Did you see the people arrested, Noa?' I nodded. 'Well,

did they look like normal members of society? Did they look like the sort of people who could source and store explosives and a lorry and drive to a highly guarded facility without appearing on any CCTV cameras or attracting police attention? And think about what you saw.'

I shuddered. That was the last thing I wanted to do.

'No, try, baby. Really think about exactly what you saw. Think of colours and objects not emotions.'

I closed my eyes and the images came back as if they were burned onto my retinas.

'Did you actually see anything other than damaged metal and red liquid?'

I shook my head. I hadn't. I actually hadn't seen any ... well *anything*.

'So ask yourself,' he continued, 'could it have all been faked?'

And there it was: a ray of hope.

Maybe it was all a lie – just a Ministry ploy to make everyone hate the Opposition. No babies had been harmed. No blood had been spilt. I had to call Jack. I had to tell him.

Dad didn't seem so keen. A look of panic came over his face. 'Best not, love,' he said, trying to give out an air of calm. 'You never know who's listening. Oh, and don't tell Mum what I said. She'll go mad if she thinks I'm filling your head with this stuff. These are the kind of ideas that can get you killed.'

Jack said it was time to cash in my modelling promise, so I went over to his to get it over and done with. The added bonus was that I got to share Dad's theory with Jack pretty quickly and it was so nice seeing him take it all in. It was as if worry lines had been rubbed out on his face. But almost instantly they reappeared. I could see the cogs turning behind his freckled forehead.

'What?'

'Think about it. If they can do this, what else can they get away with?'

I had been so caught up with feeling relieved that loads of babies probably hadn't actually been killed that I hadn't really considered this side of things. We both literally shuddered.

Then we caught each other's eyes again and started laughing. It was sometimes all so horrific you had to just laugh at the horror, like trying to exorcise a ghost or something.

'Right – take your jumper off,' Jack commanded, reaching for his sketching stuff. 'Get ready to be drawn like you've never been drawn before.' I must have looked taken aback as we both seemed to query for a sec whether that was some sort of dodgy innuendo or not. 'OK. Forget that, please. That came out a bit unfortunate. Try and do a lunge, like this.'

I attempted to copy. 'What about my face?' I asked. 'Should I be angry or happy or scared or...'

Jack interrupted. 'Don't worry – I'm not going to draw your face,' which I actually found massively insulting. I mean, I know I'm not as hot as Daisy or anything, but surely I'm not so rough that my face has to be left out? I don't even have any spots at the moment.

Jack must have caught my expression as he said, gently, 'It's not like that. You know I ... like your face. It's for your sake that's all. In case it's, the picture that is, is ... misinterpreted.'

I had to stand still, in a slight lunge pose with my left arm raised for over an hour. By the end, I had thigh cramp and my arm had severe pins and needles.

'Tense your biceps,' Jack instructed at one point. 'I want you to look powerful.' I did and then Jack repeated himself.

'I am tensing it, you idiot,' I replied laughing. 'This is as tense as my biceps get!' And then Jack sprang forward and grabbed my arm, doing an over-exaggerated examination from wrist to shoulder to check.

'Noa Blake, you are really, really weak!' he concluded and then picked me up and started twirling me around over his head, like I was some sort of ball and he was a sports jock, which I suppose he is. We collapsed on the floor laughing.

And then there was this one moment when we looked

in each other's eyes and his arms were around me and I felt so safe that I nearly kissed him and then I didn't and then the moment passed.

We stood up a bit awkwardly, neither wanting to acknowledge what hadn't quite happened and then I resumed my stupid pose and Jack picked up his charcoal again.

When he'd finished, Jack didn't want to let me see what he'd done and even started to roll the paper up. But there was no way I was going to let that happen. I pounced, unrolled the paper and then just stood there, motionless, like a calcified denser. He'd drawn a person (me with added biceps) standing defiantly whilst morphing into a robot. The head was unrecognisable, but you could clearly see a node on the neck and a wire connecting it to an out-of-shot Port. Metallic structures replaced hands and feet and the eyes were red LEDS.

A look of horror crossed my face.

'Jack ... you can't. Not for the SAM.'

'I thought you'd like it. I mean it's meant to be challenging.' His face melted from certainty into a puddle of doubt. 'I mean the whole point of Art is to make you think, isn't it? To question? And the Ministry did introduce the SAM so they must be looking for that, right?'

'What did Mrs Foster say?' I asked, quietly. 'About the idea I mean?'

'I haven't really talked it through with her. I wanted to surprise her.'

I really hope Mrs Foster can talk some sense into Jack. I mean if Mr Daniels finds a sketch of a dog too challenging, what the hell is the Ministry going to make of a none-too-subtle metaphor for freakoids?

'Promise me you'll really think about this one, Jack. And show it to Mrs Foster soon OK?'

He promised.

Some people just have rubbish luck. You know when you hear a Priest going on about how everything happens for a reason or how people deserve what they get 'cos they must have done some massive sin, well, they're just talking rubbish. If I met one I'd tell them to 'stick it up their jumper'. That's Daisy's and my new phrase. Daisy's aunt is really anti any form of swearing and would literally have an epi fit if someone said something as lame as 'damn' around her. So she makes up her own swear words and this one's so bad it's good.

Anyway, Jack is one of these super-unlucky people. His dad leaves when he's six and is then shot dead by the police, and his mum, who cares more about her boob size than her son, shacks up with a random bloke who also cares more about her boob size than her son. And now, just when everything was looking a bit hopeful, this happens.

We had double Art straight after lunch. Jack had brought his portfolio with him as promised, so that he could show that picture to Mrs Foster and (I desperately hoped) get some feedback about the massively controversial direction he was taking.

We knew something was wrong as soon as we walked into the Art room. Mr Daniels was perched on the desk next to the biggest neek you've ever seen and there was no sign of Mrs Foster.

Mr Daniels pompously motioned for us to sit down with a wave of his fat hand and then introduced, 'Mr Dreakin,' our 'new Art teacher'. Mr Dreakin nodded hello from behind his blue-tinted glasses. Super seedy. And who, other than a complete paedo, wears blue-tinted glasses anyway? His clothes were AWFUL as well. Black rubbishly cut suit, dark purple shirt and black tie. He looked like the sort of person who would wear a t-shirt with a silver spaceship on it at the weekend.

'Where's Mrs Foster?' Barnaby asked, voicing all our thoughts.

'She's left to focus on her own creative projects,' Mr Daniels replied, his lie as shiny as his over-polished front teeth. No teacher leaves just before the TAA, certainly no teacher as nice and committed as Mrs Foster.

I reached over and squeezed Jack's right hand. He was

sitting to my left, as always in Art, and I could see his eyes begin to glaze over and the muscles in his right hand begin to twitch. I was terrified that he was going to do something stupid. I only let go of his hand when Mr Daniels was safely down the corridor.

'Who's going to help with my SAM now?' Jack asked quietly.

'Maybe Mr Dreakin's actually really good.' I replied, trying to inject hope into my voice. 'Inspiring, even.'

Then Mr Dreakin set our first assignment – a scale drawing of a chair using set squares – and Jack seemed to collapse into the bench, his massive frame looking small for the first time ever.

To my surprise Raf came up to Jack at the end of the lesson. He patted his arm and said, 'I'm really sorry, mate. I know how important she was to you,' with real, totally non-sarcy concern in his voice.

Jack looked at him with such a look of pure hatred that even I drew back slightly. 'I'm not your mate. And get your freakoid hand off me,' he said as he pushed past into the corridor.

'I'm sorry,' I whispered to Raf. 'It's just this is a really big deal for him.'

Raf nodded, his eyes filled with compassion. He's really the most non-freakoidy freakoid I've ever met.

'At least he's got you,' Raf continued.

'Yes, we're really good *friends*,' I replied, blushing

furiously as I realised that I'd put way too much stress on the word friends.

And then Raf smiled and the smile widened his jaw and narrowed his eyes and he looked like a really sexy wolf.

As I walked out of the classroom, I saw Jack's latest sketch screwed up into a ball and dumped in the bin. After making sure no one was looking, I quickly removed it from the bin and stuffed it into the bottom of my bag to take home and burn.

So, big news of the day – Raf invited me back to his after school.

I was sitting on one of the benches by the main gate, chatting with Daisy and Jack, when he walked or rather strolled up and asked if I fancied studying at his. We've got this big Biology test tomorrow. Apparently his mum is 'totally cool' about him having friends over whenever. Yes – he said 'friends'. I am now officially friends with the cool blue/green-eyed boy.

Obviously I wanted to say yes, but was worried about the test. I mean how much studying could I really get done if the guy I was hanging out with just needed to upload for two minutes? And he'd think I was just some boring, slow denser if I'm there with my flashcards like the special kid.

I tried to explain this to Raf, thinking he'd laugh in my face, but he just looked embarrassed, like he'd been somehow caught out or something. I hadn't even realised he could get embarrassed as he always seems so cool. But then said he'd do the test my way – study and not upload and that way we'd be even.

A freakoid not upload! Daisy's jaw literally hit the ground and Jack nearly choked on his crisps.

Stunned, I mumbled some sort of lame acceptance and as we headed off, Daisy kept on making really embarrassing kissing sounds. I looked back at Jack and he was just staring off in a different direction, with a weird, blank look on his face.

Raf's flat is big! Raf's mum was cooking and she seemed genuinely nice and pleased to meet me. Said she'd heard all about me, at which I turned the colour of Amanda's lipstick and I swear Raf even blushed a bit too. His dad was still at work. Even when I left at 9:30pm. Raf didn't look phased by this so I guess it must be normal. I don't get the impression that they're particularly close or anything.

We spent ages revising. Cramming, testing each other and just chatting. Even his room is cool. There's a bookshelf crammed full of novels, and books on science, art and music. Not like any freakoid room I've ever seen.

Logan's room is OCD neat with no personality (just like Logan!) and Charles' room had a TV, a spotless desk and, pride of place, his Port. But Raf's desk was probably more chaotic than mine, if possible, and his Port was hidden from view behind a gravity-defying pile of books.

There were also loads of photos on the wall. There was one of Raf aged about six hugging this really pretty older girl. I felt a weird pang of jealously until I realised (1) it's perverted to think that way about a six year old and (2) the girl had an identical smile to Raf so had to be related to him. Raf must have seen what I was looking at as he nodded at the photo and said, 'That's Chloe. My sister.'

Chloe's four years older than Raf and passed her TAA with flying colours. She's now at an elite boarding school in the Second City. Raf said she's doing pretty well there. I asked him if he saw a lot of her but then he seemed to get a bit defensive. He said she'd changed a lot since he was six and made it clear he wanted to talk about something else.

I can't quite make Raf out. Tonight he seemed like he was actually pretty clever. He knew stuff way beyond the syllabus. Like that energy can be both a particle and a wave, which makes no sense to me whatsoever but is clearly quite amazing. And he knew all these really useful ways to revise. He seemed a bit weirded out when I asked him about it. I mean, what's the point when you can just upload? But he said his last school taught revision skills so I guess that explains things. I can't imagine Hollets doing anything like that, but I guess it's 85 per cent freakoid so everything is structured around their needs. Us Norms have just got to try and keep up.

After studying, Raf actually walked me home. Like an old-fashioned gentleman. I don't think even Jack would do something like that. I mean it's not like it's dangerous around here at all, in the sense of being stabbed or raped or anything. That's the one upside of a massive police presence.

When we reached my road I decided to do it. I told Raf about Daisy's party at the weekend and asked if he wanted to come. I tried to sound casual. I failed dismally. There was what seemed like the world's longest silence and I could feel this massive blush creeping up my face. I felt like crawling into the drain by the edge of the pavement I was so embarrassed.

Then Raf started laughing.

'Look at me,' he said. 'Look into my eyes,' he continued in this fake magician's voice waving his hands around in an intentionally malc way. I did, and drowned in pools of blue and green. 'I would love to come to Daisy's party with you.'

'Not with me.' I floundered. 'I wasn't asking you out or anything.'

'Well, then I'd love to go to Daisy's party without you.'

And then he laughed again, hugged me and walked off. He didn't look back. Which was lucky as I had this really malc grin on my face and must have looked like a right denser staring after him.

Call-me-Marcus was on duty outside my apartment block. He smiled as he recognised me walking up the steps. 'Good night then, love?' he asked.

'The best,' I replied with a stupid smile on my face. 'Just the best.'

I wanted to call Daisy as soon as I got home to tell her all about it, but Mum and Dad were in the living room so I'd have had to practically sit next to them and they'd have heard EVERY word. It's malc sharing a phone. Mum has a mobile for emergencies, but as a mere mortal without a special Ministry licence, I don't get to touch one. And they're bound to monitor calls so they'd know if I borrowed hers. I'll tell Daisy first thing tomorrow.

I've just realised why Jack was mad at me. I was supposed to be helping him revise Biology, the last of the three big science tests. He always does better if I study with him and explain it again. I hope he forgives me by tomorrow.

The Biology test was pretty hard and I could see Jack sitting, head in hands, stylus hovering mid-air through the second section.

As Mr Hanson called time and we all filed out of the classroom, I managed to weasel my way to Jack's side and squeeze his hand. He stiffened and gave me a token nod, the sort of thing you'd do to a kid of a family friend you weren't massively keen on but couldn't just blatantly ignore.

'I'm really sorry about last night,' I mumbled. 'I completely forgot and I feel terrible.'

'Well that's all OK then, isn't it,' Jack shot back. 'You promise to help me. You don't. I fail. But you're *sorry*.' He literally spat out the last word, like it was a particularly grim piece of mucor stew. 'Do you want me to be a Fish, is that it?' he continued, furiously. '''Cos that's sure the way you're acting. Get me out the way so there are no distractions from freakoid lover-boy?' Jack's right hand was now a fist and pulsing.

I saw Raf out the corner of my eye, looking concerned and about to approach, so I desperately signalled him away with my eyes and tried a bit of telepathic channelling too. Raf swerved and kept walking. I got nothing in the way of telepathic reply though so that's a 'no' to my having that particular talent.

Just then Daisy waltzed over and wrapped one arm round each of us, joining us in an awkward sort of triangle.

'Why are my best friends fighting?' she demanded. I remained silent.

'Noa broke her promise,' Jack muttered.

'Jack called Raf a freakoid,' I countered lamely.

Daisy rolled her eyes melodramatically. 'So we're in Kindergarten now are we? Jack – grow up. You need to learn to study by yourself. Noa – stop being a crap friend and by the way, Raf is a freakoid. And we're having a party on Saturday that I'm not going to let you guys ruin. Now hug as if you mean it.' And Daisy had us hugging again and again in the corridor and repeating, 'I forgive you,' until she was truly satisfied and we were all laughing. We got some odd looks and more than a couple of, 'Uhhhh Fish losers,' in the process.

Knights don't all wear shining armour. Some even wear police uniform.

The day started badly. Mum announced that Uncle Pete might be coming to stay. Dad and I immediately let out massive groans. I am so embarrassed to be related to Uncle Pete. He's supposed to be intelligent and everything, as he has some highish-up job in the Ministry doing something to do with statistics, but he has no social skills and offends absolutely everyone, me included. I mean he once told Jack that they had identified the 'ginger gene' and everyone who used a WombPod could choose to exclude it at embryo selection stage. 'Which of course they all do!' Guffaw, guffaw, guffaw. Idiot.

I started ranting at Mum and Dad why couldn't we have any decent relatives other than Ella (and sometimes, depending on mood, Auntie Vicki)? Dad said nothing but started putting on his coat to leave for work even though he didn't actually have to go for another ten minutes and Mum shot evil looks at me.

'What?' I asked. Sometimes I think Mum forgets that I don't have the same telepathic connection that she and Dad seem to.

Her expression softened. 'Sorry, love. It's just that you know Dad's really sensitive about any talk about relatives because of Uncle Max. It's hard for him, you know.'

I nodded but I don't know really. I just know Dad had a brother who died before I was born and I'm not allowed to ask about it and if I ever try to, Dad just seems to go into standby mode.

Anyway, this conversation, if you can call it that, meant I was late leaving for school and would have to run at least some of the way. I hurtled down the steps leading from our block on to the pavement and managed to run slap into the police witch who'd made me search through my garbage before. I mumbled an apology and thought there was no way she'd stop me this time as I had my Hollets uniform on and everything. I was wrong.

'Please state your name.' Her voice was ice.

'Noa Blake,' I replied, trying to avoid eye contact, trying to appear submissive.

'Empty your bag,' came her next command. I couldn't believe it. Not again. Not when I clearly just had a school bag and was clearly running because I was clearly late for school. It wasn't as if I was smuggling loads of subversive materials to some top secret Opposition meeting. But then it struck me. At the bottom of my bag was Jack's scrunched-up picture. The one that could be 'misinterpreted'. The one I'd forgotten to burn. My heart started to hammer and I was this terrible level of awake. Colours became more intense and all the energy in my body was buzzing around my legs. I opened my mouth but no words came out. It was like the dream in which I find out the TAA is actually a spoken test and I've turned mute so I fail. I'm terrible at hiding my feelings and a look of pure panic must have zipped across my face. The witch started to smile, as if she knew she was going to catch me with something terrible and get to ruin my life.

I was just deciding whether it'd be better to try and run or to eat the picture, when I saw the squat figure of Marcus approaching.

'What's up here, Officer Hicks?' Marcus asked, nodding at me.

'Standard stop and search procedures.'

'We'll let this one go, I think. She seems pretty harmless.' And then he winked at me and tapped me on the shoulder with his baton. 'Now off with you, love, and hurry. Don't want you costing your family any rations, now do we.'

And it's the rare times when something like this happens, or I remember that the police have their share of Marcuses, that I think maybe the Territory isn't such a bad place to live after all.

I hate Hugo Barnes. I really, really hate him.

We got our Biology test results back today. Mr Hanson read them out to the class.

Jack got 45 per cent. He tried to look like he was OK about it and even did a hilarious fish impression, but I could tell he was pretty worried. I mean it's now only five weeks till the TAA and there's no way that 45 per cent is ever going to be a pass, even with a SAM.

Daisy got 67 per cent, which was better than normal, but still not safe, and her mum always goes super-stressy at anything under 75 per cent. Raf got 83 per cent which was amazingly about what he'd got in the last Geography test that he uploaded for. Jack got really moody and said that Raf would just have uploaded after I left. I wish he'd give Raf a chance.

Hugo got 89 per cent and was looking pretty smug (normal freakoid facial expression) until Mr Hanson read out my result. 92 per cent – in your face, Hugo Barnes!! Apparently Hugo (along with nearly every other freakoid) had done better than me in the recall fact section, but I'd whooped him in the 'apply your knowledge' part.

You could tell immediately that Hugo was NOT HAPPY. His mean, ice-blue eyes narrowed and a muscle under his left cheekbone started to twitch. Amanda couldn't help herself and reached over to stroke his arm, but Hugo shoved her away.

Mr Hanson chose that moment to leave the room to photocopy some sheets.

Hugo walked up to my bench, pushed my stuff onto the floor and called me a stupid, cheating Norm. This I could handle and I just laughed at him. I'd worked really hard for that test and had beaten him fair and square. This seemed to wind him up even more and that's when it all went wrong. Hugo said I didn't deserve to be at Hollets, that all Norms should be shipped off to the Wetlands at birth as they were like a sub-species. He said the Laboratory should never have employed my mum and that her decision to carry me, 'like a fat whale', and not to use a WombPod like every other government employee made her an embarrassment to the Territory. He said that he'd personally pay to have me and my 'saggy' mum shipped off to the Wetlands today.

When he started on about my mum, that's when I saw red. My mum's one of the good guys. One of the very few properly, truly, good guys. Through her research she saves lives every day. I wanted to scream at him and hit him but

I knew he'd like that, so I pretended like I wasn't fazed and then did what I knew would provoke him most. I stood up slowly and jerked my arms around chanting, 'My-name-is Hugo-Barnes-and-I-am-a-freakoid-robot-with-no-natural-intelligence.'

Suddenly I noticed that the room had gone really quiet. I turned around to see Mr Daniels standing in the doorway. I could tell by his expression that he'd seen everything. I've got to go and see him in his office on Monday.

He said nothing to Hugo of course.

I hate Hugo Barnes.

I guess we should have known that they'd find out about Daisy's party. We'd been inviting other Norms (and the occasional OK freakoid such as Barnaby) in the lunch hall and they must have overheard or something.

I find it hard to believe that I was ever friends with Amanda or that Jack and Hugo used to be pretty close at junior school. Hugo used to play football with Jack basically every Sunday morning and Amanda even came to my first sleepover. My friendship with Amanda, and Jack's with Hugo, all changed when we got to ten. They suddenly stopped wanting anything to do with us and we didn't exactly want to hang out with them either as they became super annoying. Mum said Amanda just hit puberty early. And I know she became absurdly guy-orientated, but it was more than that. She only liked freakoids; started to listen in class; blanked me. Now they're so bloody superior and they just have to wreck everything.

Anyway, about 9pm the party was starting to get fun and people were actually dancing in the lounge. We'd moved the sofas to the edge of the room so there was a kind of dance floor and Daisy had put little tealights all along the mantelpiece to create a 'romantic' atmosphere. I think she thought it might help me to get it properly together with Raf! Jack was in a really good mood and he's hilarious when he dances as he's so big. A dance move that you might not notice in anyone else is magnified by his massive body into something totally absurd. He kept pulling this one particular move – sort of hammering with his right hand and bending his knees in time with the music. He looked like a genuine denser. Then he kept on trying to dance with me and hook his arm round my waist, but it didn't feel right and I remained glued to a sofa at the edge.

'Why are you being off with me?' he asked, but I didn't feel like having THAT conversation so I pretended I was hungry and went to eat some crisps I really wasn't in the mood for.

My eyes kept returning to the front door, my heart

getting a weird lame flutter every time someone new walked in. The flutter turned manic when Raf finally turned up just after 9pm. He was wearing this yellow shirt that would have looked malc on anyone else but somehow looked really cool on him. Jack must have seen my reaction as he said, 'Oh, OK, I get it. I see,' before stomping off. I was torn between approaching Raf and following Jack when the doorbell rang one more time.

Daisy, euphoric from dancing and general flirting, sprang up to open the door, her dazzling hostess smile at the ready. The smile vanished and I knew something was wrong.

Hugo and Quentin barged in. Here comes trouble, we all thought, but they were acting nice. Worryingly nice. They'd brought loads of bottles of vodka with them and without it seeming like they had any sort of agenda, the vodka was made into cocktails and before long everyone was pretty hammered.

I'd only had two drinks but was already feeling a bit out of it. I remember edging round one side of the sofa to get back to where Raf was, when Hugo sneaked round the other side. Quentin blocked the way back and I was caught in an evil freakoid sandwich. Quentin started to stroke my arm in a pretty sleazy way and Hugo just watched and laughed as if he was properly enjoying it, but not in a fancying me way, more in a 'I like to watch her suffer' way.

'Stop it,' I hissed. I didn't want Raf, or Jack for that matter, to clock what was going on, as I knew there'd just be a massive fight and things would get out of hand.

Quentin stayed put. His hand kept moving, roughly now. He kept on trying to put it down the V of my top.

'Get your pervy hand off me.' I pushed him away.

'Stop pretending you don't like it,' laughed Hugo. 'Have another drink. Everyone knows Norms are easy. Why do you think we came to this malc party?'

Quentin grabbed my wrists, pinning them behind my back with one of his massive hands.

'Get off!' I shouted, a lot louder this time. Everyone in the room stared at us.

I must have gone a bit trancey. I was brought back into the room with a start at the THUMP as someone's head hit the wall. I turned to see Raf trying to tackle Hugo. His face looked calm but his eyes were blue and green ice. Hugo had the weight advantage though so Raf kept on being thrown to the floor and the best he could manage was to jump onto Hugo's back and end up having a kind of piggy back. The absurdity of it made me giggle in spite of myself. That is, until I saw Jack, his face distilled anger, wrenching Quentin's arms behind his back as he repeated slammed his head against the wall. I don't know if he'd broken Quentin's nose, but blood was streaming out of it and there was a trail, like train tracks, down the pale green wallpaper.

'Jack, stop!' Daisy shouted, seeing it at the same time. 'He's not worth it.'

We both rushed over to Jack and tried to pull him off Quentin. It was like ants trying to stop a truck. I tried again, grabbing Jack's left arm and he instinctively punched back hard, throwing me off. My head seemed to crunch as I hit the edge of the coffee table. The metallic taste of blood in my mouth. Then blackness.

People with 'self-inflicted' injuries don't get to go to hospital. Can't even see a doctor. Well, I guess you could see a private one, but even if you could afford that, there'd still be records. Carelessness and risk-taking are BAD personality traits. Show a lack of judgement. As does mixing with violent citizens. So, even though you're a victim, you're not worth saving. Getting hurt at a party, doesn't matter whose fault it was, counts as 'self-inflicted'. Guess the top Ministry peeps didn't get many invitations when they were young.

Apparently I blacked out as soon as I'd hit the table. Daisy had called Mum and Dad immediately. She knew an ambulance wouldn't come and that if she called one, we'd probably both be put under surveillance.

Everyone apart from Raf, Daisy and Jack had left when

they arrived. Daisy said Dad took one look at my head and Jack's hand and told him to, 'Get out, while you still can.' I can't quite believe it. Dad's a big fan of Jack's. But I suppose he did (accidentally) deck his baby girl. Then Dad lifted me over his shoulder 'like a sack of potatoes' (thanks Daisy – maybe like 'sleeping beauty' would have been nicer!) and carried me all the way home.

Mum's science training and medical supplies came in useful. She gave me something for the pain, bathed the cut (luckily above the hairline so I won't get a grimbo face scar) and kept me awake to check it hadn't hurt my brain and turned me into a genuine denser. I actually began to enjoy it. I felt the most secure and cocooned I had for ages. Felt the stresses of the world and the endless revision and the exam just slip away. I think the drugs were pretty strong.

Mum made me stay in bed the whole day and wouldn't even let me revise, didn't want me to strain my head! We laughed about it. Never, when I was little, would I have thought I'd be pushing my mum to let me study more. Please, just one more chapter of Physics – pretty please!

I had visitors all afternoon. It was better than a birthday.

First Daisy, filling me in on all the details. Like how Hugo and Quentin had just fled as soon as I'd been punched out. How Raf had gazed 'all gooey eyed' on my limp body. (Cool.) And how Jack had almost gone into a state of shock at what he'd done. And how she'd had to spend the rest of the night (with Raf's help – he's so great!) cleaning up; trying to tidy up any breakages and remove bloodstains. Daisy was trying to pretend it was all OK and just really funny, but I could tell she was seriously stressing. One of her mum's prized tacky glass sculptures had been shattered and Daisy hadn't been able to completely get the blood off the wallpaper. In the end they'd pulled a sofa in front of it as a lame disguise, so hopefully her Mum won't move it and go mental when she gets back in five hours time.

Raf dropped round at about 3pm, but massively annoyingly I'd just fallen asleep again so didn't get to see him. Even worse, Mum hadn't realised I was asleep and had shown him into my room and I'd been snoring. How unattractive is that!?!

Jack sheepishly appeared just before dinner. His face was all puffy and it looked like he'd been crying although he totally denied it.

'I'm so sorry, Noa,' he said, and his voice was regret itself. 'I can't believe I hurt you. I didn't see you there. I just see red and then … it's like my fists control themselves. I know that sounds lame, but that's what happens. Honestly.'

'Don't worry – I know what you're like. I know it was an accident. How's Quentin?'

'Dunno. I think I broke his nose.'

'Poor Daisy. Lucky Raf was there to help her clean up.'

'Well, he did start it.'

I couldn't quite believe what Jack was saying.

'He basically jumped Hugo and caused the whole fight.'

'Jack. You are unbelievable. They came to get us drunk and perv on Norms. Quentin was feeling me up. Just get out, Jack. Get out.'

I was so upset I nearly forgot about having to see Mr Daniels tomorrow. Nearly.

Mr Daniels is a nasty man with too much power and now he's out to ruin my life.

I made sure I got to his office first thing as he has a real issue about being on time. I knocked and he made me wait ages before saying I could come in. I don't think he was actually busy – it just made him feel important.

It's the first time I've been in his office. It was weird. I know from hearing other teachers talk that he's got a family and stuff but there weren't any pictures of them on his wall or on his desk. The only photo was of him fawning over the Education Minister. It was embarrassing.

Anyway, he gave me his most serious 'I'm disappointed in you' look and asked if there was anything I wanted to say.

I know I should just have apologised and grovelled and

everything, but looking at him and his tragic hair plugs and his smug, fat face, I just couldn't do it.

'Hugo Barnes started it,' I began.

Mr Daniels didn't listen of course. He just pompously raised one hand.

'I'm very disappointed in you, Noa Blake,' he said. 'Hollets is a rare and special school in that, unlike many of its peers, it opens its doors to the less-evolved members of our society.' (I nearly choked here – I can't believe he actually said that to my face. And anyway it's 85 per cent freakoids so the door's clearly not open very wide. And he's a Norm himself although he seems to have conveniently forgotten this fact!) He went on to say that my 'deplorable antics' (antics!?! – it was just a robot dance!!) lent weight to the argument that there was no place for Norms at a place like Hollets.

Now this is the worst bit. He then looked me directly in the eye and I'm sure I saw a glimpse of a smile on his lips. He was actually enjoying this. 'I have no choice in these circumstances, but to give you a formal caution.'

My head reeled. New Ministry regs meant that a formal caution now automatically meant the deduction of two points from your final TAA mark.

'But that's two points,' I cried out. 'How can that be fair?!'

His mouth was a thin grey line.

'I don't set the penalties, Noa. And if you ever speak to

me in that insubordinate manner again you will lose a lot more than two points.'

It took all my self-control to remain silent.

But still: two points. Two whole points!! Hugo Barnes gets nothing and I lose two points. Two points can easily be the difference between a pass and a fail. But Mr Daniels just sat there as if he'd just given me a detention or asked me to pick up litter. Does his miniscule brain not register he might have given me a death sentence? Or does he get some sort of perverse kick out of playing God like this?

'You, student of ant-like importance, I sentence you to die a slow and miserable death of starvation and disease, now please turn to page twenty-four of your text book and copy out the section on inert gases.'

I don't know what I'm going to tell my mum. She's going to go mental.

I told Daisy and she tried to cheer me up, saying I'd be fine and my marks were good enough anyway, but I could tell by the way she started curling her hair with her finger that she was properly worried for me. I avoided Raf. I saw him hanging around by the main entrance where we'd arranged to meet so I slipped out the side door. I think he saw me. I know it's not his fault but I couldn't really handle seeing any freakoids now, even him. I mean he was caught openly laughing at Mr Daniel's hair in Assembly and gets away with an off-the-books bollocking. Jack's right. It's all so massively unfair.

It was Jack's shoulder I really wanted to cry on, but things are so messed up between us. Why can't everything just be simple? Like it used to be.

I take back what I once said. The Territory is a terrible place to live.

We went to see Aunty Vicki and my cousin Ella today.

It took ages to get there. There weren't many other cars as electricity's so heavily rationed, but Aunty Vicki and Ella live right at the edge of the Territory so it's never quick. Mum gets extra rations anyway in case she needs to get to some terrible disease outbreak quickly.

Aunty Vicki always jokes that you can see the mosquito grids and hear the cries of the Wetlanders (Fish) from their top window. Then we say, 'What do they sound like?' and she takes a big gulp of water and gargles and says 'Gulp, gulp' at the same time and manages to snort some of the water out of her nose. I know it sounds lame, but it's actually pretty hilarious. And difficult. I tried it once at home but snorted the water down my windpipe instead and literally couldn't breathe for two minutes. Drowning would be really rubbish. I should write that on a Post-it and stick it above my revision timetable. A *motivational aid*. Dad got me this really lame book about 'how to revise' and there was a whole chapter on 'motivational aids'. It was pretty dense. You don't exactly get skivers anymore.

Living next to the Wetlands isn't that hilarious for Aunty Vicki and Ella though. Occasionally they're woken at night by the sirens, massively powerful searchlights and the staccato of machine-gun fire, if some poor Wetlander decides it's all too much and tries to scale the Fence. They're usually firing at dead bodies, the fence being electric and everything. There's been less and less mention of any of this recently though. Ella's sitting the TAA this year too so I guess it's all a bit more real now.

Ella rushed out to meet us and gave me a massive hug and sort of ruffled my hair. She always acts like she's my big sister or something, even though she's only three months older than me. Aunty Vicki waited inside the house. She gave me a hug in the hall but just sort of nodded at Mum. I mean she said all the right things, but there was no real warmth there. Which is really sad 'cos Mum always says they were really close when they were young. There's a picture on our mantelpiece of them with their arms wrapped round each other, matching tragic fringes and gappy teeth.

We sat outside in their tiny paved square. They've turned all the rest of their garden into a vegetable plot. Food's scarce out here. But the vegetables didn't look so good. Lots had greyish-yellow leaves. 'Grey rot,' Aunty Vicki said. 'Apparently the soil is too wet. And salty.' And then she did this weird sort of little laugh, all brittle and harsh and we didn't really know whether we should be joining in or not, 'cos it wasn't funny. At least Dad managed a chuckle and Aunty Vicki seemed to thaw a fraction of a degree. He always gets it right.

Mum and Aunty Vicki started getting on a bit better until school got mentioned.

It's a massive issue between them. That I'm going to Hollets and Ella's stuck at Swithin's (a right dump).

'How's school?' Aunty Vicki asked and the temperature literally dropped about five degrees. I moronically started talking about my new friend Raf.

'Raf?' Aunty Vicki practically jumped down my throat. 'That's a pretty posh name for a Norm.'

My silence said everything.

'Let it go, Vic,' said Mum.

But she couldn't. 'What, so it's not enough that your daughter is going to Hollets, she's now got to make friends with Childes too? I'm surprised you deign to even visit us. We are so beneath you now.'

It's like she blames Mum. Like Mum's massively immoral for taking up a place that the Ministry pays for. I asked Mum about it once and she said that Aunty Vicki thinks that she should quit the Laboratory as the system is so unfair. But Mum's doing good work. She helps with disease prevention and everything. Mum just turned away and looked embarrassed when I said this.

'I'm no saint, Noa,' she said. But she's just being modest.

I hung out with Ella in her room. She has a massive print of Kaio above her bed. He is just the coolest. Mum would only let me put up prints of animals or maps or something equally lame which would obviously be much more embarrassing than nothing, so I have nothing on my walls. I saw Ella's school files stacked on a bookcase. I had a rant about how boring I found Geography and how hard I found Trigonometry. Ella looked at me blankly. 'Trigonometry,' I repeated, afraid that I'd pronounced it wrong and looked like a complete denser. Ella seemed to shrink a bit and said they hadn't done that. Which is really weird as it's a major part of the Maths paper. Ella said that they hadn't done a lot.

They did a lot of other stuff, like survival skills. She can purify water using a muslin and iodine tablets, identify five types of edible seaweed and light a fire using two dry sticks. Which is cool and everything but…

'In case we fail,' Ella said quietly. I felt sick. I mean she's not even got the chance to try. How could she beat me, let alone a freakoid, if she's not even learning Trig? Ella's actually really clever. She gets things (and agrees that Uncle Pete is horrific, which is an excellent indicator). They're just preparing her to be shipped off.

Ella said that Aunty Vicki's trying to help her study after work every day. But often she finishes late. She has to work long shifts now that Uncle John isn't around anymore.

'It's not so bad,' Ella said. 'Mum's going to come too. And your mum's going to help us out with malarial tablets and stuff.'

'Don't talk like that. It's not going to happen,' I tried to reassure her. 'I'm sure you'll pass.' But we both heard how fake my voice sounded.

There was an awkward silence.

'Let's not talk about it any more.' Ella said. 'Since when do we ever talk about school anyway? Let's talk about guys.' And then she launched into far, far too much detail about some guy called Matt who she's sort of off and on with and who likes to walk around with his hand around the back of her neck, which if you ask me, shows he's clearly a bit of a psycho.

'Now it's your turn.' Ella looked at me eagerly. 'Have you snogged Jack yet? Have you conquered the ginger mountain?'

I gave an exasperated sort of 'Aggghhh. How many times do I have to tell you? WE'RE JUST FRIENDS.'

Ella laughed so much she looked like she might pee herself just a little. She loves winding me up. Then she sat up all serious and asked, 'You're not really friends with a freakoid, are you?'

'He's not like the other ones. He's … he's cool.'

'Yeah, right!'

'No, he is. He's interesting and funny and has these really amazing eyes that change colour, well, not change obviously as that would be impossible, but seem to change if he winks, which he does a lot.'

'Oh, God. You've actually fallen for a freakoid, haven't you!' Ella sounded properly shocked. She wasn't winding me up this time. 'You do know that it'll just be some sort of sick game to him, don't you. "Hey let's snog a Norm. See what it's like while some my age are still around." It's probably for a bet.'

'He's not like that.'

'They're all like that.'

'Do you actually know any?'

'What, you mean because I'm at some rubbish school and not good enough to mix with them?'

And then we both looked at each other and realised that we sounded exactly like Mum and Aunty Vicki.

It was time to go and I felt really bad about leaving Ella with things being rubbish and tense. We've never argued before and that's probably the last time I'll see her before the exam. I made Dad stop the car at the end of the drive and I sprinted back and just hugged Ella goodbye again, properly this time.

'Good luck! Stay dry,' I said, furiously blinking away tears.

'Good luck! Stay dry,' she repeated, eyes wet too.

During the drive back I asked Mum and Dad if there was anything we could do to help Ella. I mean it's so unfair. They looked at each other before talking. They do this sort of telepathic agreeing thing before talking about something serious. I wish I knew how it worked.

Then they just shook their heads. We didn't have any money spare. If it wasn't for the free place, I'd be at some dump school too. Even Dad's salary as a family lawyer wouldn't cut it. He'd have to be doing humungo deals rather than wills and probate to pay Hollets' fees.

Mum said that Aunty Vicki would go too if it came to it. Make sure Ella was safe.

'In a way, Ella's lucky,' Mum said. I nearly choked. Yeah, real lucky.

Raf is complicated. Good complicated, I guess, but complicated nonetheless.

He came round to mine to study this evening. By some horrific bit of bad luck on my part, both Mum and Dad were back from work and so I had to do the whole 'meet the parents' thing. Raf was great with them – really polite but still natural and totally himself rather than some phoney creep version. Mum seemed to like him immediately, although she tried a bit overly hard at first and did massively exaggerated smiles like she was auditioning for mime school or something.

Dad was outwardly completely friendly, but I could see

he was still trying to figure Raf out, work out what some freakoid might want with his precious daughter. I was kind of pleased about that. Dad's always distrusted freakoids that bit more than Mum. I think it was him who was totally adamant that I was going to be born a Norm. 'No one is messing with my beautiful daughter's head.' Go Dad!

He ruined it a bit though with his, 'Well, I suppose you want to go and *study* now,' as if it were some massive innuendo for drop down and do it on my bedroom floor. We escaped to my room. Dad insisted we left the door open though, which again made me turn scarlet with embarrassment and Raf shake with laughter.

Anyway, as practice for the analytical writing section of the English exam we had to write a 500 word essay on how well the introduction of the TAA solved our problems in the aftermath of the Great Flood. Upside – this was a section in which you had to actually structure an answer so the freakoids didn't have an advantage. Downside – although in English there's not supposed to be a right answer, in the exam there definitely was one one that basically said everything about the Territory and the TAA was just AMAZING!

When I talk to Jack or Daisy about the TAA, the conversation always goes the same way. We agree that (1) it's massively cruel to send any fifteen year old to their pretty much guaranteed death and (2) it's massively unfair that freakoids have this huge advantage and that the test is nearly all about recall and facts rather than ideas or expression.

With Raf it was different. He sat on the floor. We both did. He said he finds it more comfortable and I didn't want to tower over him and give him an unflattering view of my thighs pressed onto a chair. (Daisy's advice.)

'So, this is such a great essay!' I laughed, automatically assuming Raf would join in. 'The TAA is the purrrrrrrfect solution to all our problems.'

Before I had time to worry that I'd somehow morphed into Daisy, Raf replied, 'It might not be the worst.'

I was silent, stunned, betrayed. Was he no different from every other freakoid after all?

'So the TAA is OK then, is it? "The best we can do"? SERIOUSLY?!? It's OK that in June thousands of Norms are going to die, is it? It's OK that my cousin and probably my friends and probably me are going to be dragged from our homes and dumped in a malarial swampland? That's great, isn't it? That's just such a great system.'

By now I was standing, angry. I didn't care how chunky my thighs looked from his angle, I kind of hated him right now.

Raf remained calm as ever and gave me one of his most hypnotising blue/green gazes.

'Noa, that's not what I meant and if you calm down for one minute… OK, obviously I phrased that badly. The

TAA is horrific. I just meant no one's come up with a good solution and some have come up with even more terrible ones. What do you know about what happens in other countries?'

I must have looked like a right confused denser as I assumed this was some sort of trick question. Everyone did the same as us, didn't they? We'd never studied it at school, never talked about it at home (and it's not as if there's any way of just looking stuff up other than through Dad's massively out-dated encyclopaedia from the stone age), but I'd know if there were other ways, wouldn't I?

Apparently not. Raf had found out by accident. His dad was working at his computer – laboratory heads are treated like top Ministry peeps: they get their own computer, even at home, database access and everything. But they have to keep them in a locked room, password protected, far from the eyes of the 'common people'. Anyway, Raf's dad had got distracted, went downstairs to have a fight with Raf's mum or something. Raf says they fight a lot.

Raf wouldn't tell me what he'd searched for. The most he'd reveal was something about how uploads work and studies from other countries (which seems like the weirdest thing ever to search for if you've suddenly got access to massive amounts of information, but hey) when he'd come across information about other countries' ways of killing off their population. And it wasn't pretty.

'The States do the same as us. We basically nicked their system. Brazil, which lost less land in the floods, has a lottery system. Everyone gets entered and if your number comes up you get sent to the flooded west coast, which is also pretty much like a death sentence. There are no freakoids in Brazil. No company bought the technology as without the test there was no real demand for it.'

'I wouldn't mind a world without freakoids.' I said. 'You excepted, of course. And at least everyone's got an equal chance of staying safe.'

But then, as Raf pointed out, some of Brazil's most intelligent and gifted scientists, thinkers and writers had been lost to their Wetlands and that had hurt its recovery. One guy who was sent was just about to crack a new form of fusion that could have released more energy than ten fission power stations and create no radioactive waste at the same time.

'Well they should have kept him, obviously,' I interrupted.

'But that wouldn't have been fair, would it? To have one rule for some and another for others? I mean a 'freakoid' is more likely than your cousin to solve our energy problems, just because they've got more information in their head and have been taught more. Does that mean it's better to ship her off?'

I had no answer for that.

'What about somewhere else then. What about France?'

'They kill older people instead. Compulsory euthanasia for the over 40s. But they're looking to change their system. Seems that if people know they're not going to live that long, they act more wildly and have loads of kids to sort of continue their legacy. France's population's massively expanding at the moment.'

'What about Australia?' I asked quietly.

'Oh, there you just have to buy a space. If you can't, you're sent to the desert zones. So there's no test – you've just got to be rich.'

'India?'

'I don't know. My dad came back in before I could find out any more and went mental. He broke my finger.' Raf said it like it was a joke, but I'm not sure it was.

'Why do you think they don't tell us this stuff?' I asked. 'Surely it'd be good for the Ministry if they could show other countries doing horrific things?'

'That's what I thought too, at first,' Raf agreed. 'But, then I realised … they don't want us to compare, to question, 'cos we might keep questioning. They just want us to accept and obey.'

'But all of this, it still doesn't make the TAA right,' I said.

'No, it doesn't,' Raf agreed. 'I hate this system. More than you can know. But it's not simple either. And if you really want to attack something you need to be able to bury your anger, to look at it coldly. To decide exactly what's wrong with it and why and then destroy that.'

And there was something about the way he said 'destroy' that sent a surge of adrenaline through me.

Oh, my God! My mum just slapped me, and I'm talking a full whack across my face. She never hits any one. She believes 'violence breeds violence'. Or at least she did. My cheek stung and I brought my hand up in shock, tears forming in the corner of my eyes.

At registration, Ms Jones handed us all these bottles of the foulest-smelling insect repellent. She said, in her best fake hushed voice, that some government spod had just discovered that a few mosquitoes carrying the Milo virus had entered the Territory from the Wetlands. We therefore have to coat ourselves in this rank yellowish fluid to protect ourselves from 'bleeding eyes, body sores and immuno-breakdown'. Nice. Apparently mosquitoes find young people's blood particularly delicious! She also banged on about how we had to protect each other as this virus is like some super-powered bug and can spread really quickly. 'One rotten apple can destroy the basket,' she said.

She's always so melodramatic. They all are. Just to make you think that you're really lucky to be in the Territory. It's bound to be lies too. We all know there are massively high electric grids between the Wetlands and Territory ready to zap any evil bug-carrying flies. Also she's just such a hypocrite. Always saying we need to protect each other but then thinking it's OK in June to turn half of us into Fish who are bound to die from this evil bug thing anyway.

Well, it only took ninety minutes till first break for Amanda to rinse the stuff off in the loos. I guess she thought it might put the amaaaaaaazing Hugo off. Yeah, like he's interested in her anyway! Thought she'd have learnt that his thing seems to be watching Norms getting groped at parties. I thought about rinsing mine off as it kept on nearly making me gag, but Jack and Daisy kept theirs on and Raf said that Amanda was an idiot for doing it. Raf looked pretty cool today. He wore a greeny-blue jumper that really brought out the green of his green eye and the blue of his blue eye.

When I got home I told my mum about the repellent and Amanda and she started doing her super-straight back thing. I said I had nearly washed the stuff off it was so grim and that's when she slapped me. Said I must never, never do anything so 'damn bloody stupid' and stormed out of the room crying. She never normally swears either.

Maybe she's going through the menopause. Daisy's mum is going through the menopause and keeps getting even more stressy than normal, if that's actually possible.

Mum apologised later. That was even scarier though. She sat next to me on my bed and kept stroking my hair saying over and over again how I must never ever wash the repellent off.

Raf doesn't upload. And he kissed me.

I can't quite believe it, either part, but it's true, both parts. And I can't tell anyone about it. I swore I wouldn't.

I spent the afternoon at Raf's again. We didn't have any major homework for tomorrow other than obviously to revise as if our lives depended on it (ha ha), so we were just talking and listening to music. I thought I could study later, all night if necessary, I just wanted to spend some time with Raf now. Then he put on Kaio and I told him about how we'd danced to it at Daisy's and then got really embarrassed as I realised how lame that sounded. I mean that's what ten-year-olds do.

Raf smiled that sexy smile he does sometimes. The smile that turns his eyes to slits and widens his jaw. Like I said, it makes him look a bit like a wolf, which shouldn't be sexy, but it is.

'I'd like to see your dancing,' he laughed.

I told him that I looked like a denser when I danced. That he should see Daisy dance.

Raf gave me one of his sideways looks. 'If I wanted to see Daisy dance, don't you think I would have invited

Daisy round? You're far sexier than Daisy and it's even sexier that you don't even know it.'

Then before I could even get one of my awful red blushes out, Raf had jumped up, turned the volume up and started doing these weird shaking jumps. Dancing like he was electrocuted. 'Are you embarrassed?' he shouted. 'Is your dancing worse than this? I bet it's worse than this.'

I couldn't help myself. I joined in. And then we had a competition as to who could do the worst dance to the track while the other commentated like on sport on TV.

'And here representing the First City in Free Style Dance is our very own Noa Blake...' he'd say and then I'd dance out from behind his curtain trying to look as ridiculous as possible.

We were laughing so much at one point that we both collapsed onto his swivel chair and that's when he kissed me. And we didn't bump teeth. And he tasted of gum rather than melted cheese. And it was amazing.

But mid-kiss the chair swivelled into the desk, crashing over the pile of books that had sat there, and exposing his Port and the wires leading to it. Which were cut.

We stopped laughing and the room seemed really silent despite the booming music.

'You can't tell anyone,' Raf said – quiet, serious, frightened.

I nodded, confused and scared too. I didn't know what was going on, but I knew it was a big deal. That something momentous had just happened, but I was too much of a denser to grasp exactly what it was. Then we sat on the floor and he started to tell me everything.

It all began with his sister, Chloe. Raf and Chloe had been really close when he was much younger. Not quite like friends as she was that bit older, but he really looked up to her and she protected him. She was a Childe as well and started uploading aged nine like every other Childe. They can't upload earlier as the nervous connections aren't fully formed and the tissue around the Node is still growing. As Chloe began to upload, Raf started to notice her change. It was very gradual, he said. His parents didn't see it and none of her friends saw it as they were changing too. But Raf noticed. It was the little things. She didn't laugh as much. She stopped making up songs; stopped impersonating the teachers; stopped making her own clothes. Instead she stayed in, studied, had clone friends and clone interests and stopped questioning anything. Raf's parents told him he was being silly. That Chloe was 'becoming a woman' or something equally cringeworthy and parent-like. But Raf decided that he wouldn't let it happen to him. He wouldn't upload and let them alter his thoughts. Make him into a human robot.

Suddenly everything that I'd noticed about Amanda and Hugo and all the other freakoids seemed to tie in as well. My dad's original fears seem to have been realised. Uploading information was one thing, but having your whole mind controlled… You'd be thinking you were uploading some facts about Noble Gases in Chemistry, but at the same time you'd be learning to always obey authority and that Norms were a sub-species. I felt sick.

'So that's what you were trying to search for on your dad's computer?'

Raf nodded.

'But why aren't they more identical then?' I probed, wanting Raf to be wrong. 'Why's Amanda so boy-obsessed? Why's Barnaby quite nice while Hugo's so awful?'

'Look, I'm not claiming to have all the answers, Noa. This is just something I've been piecing together. I guess, they can't control every element of what makes you you. God, I don't think anyone really knows exactly how personality comes about. I think they just upload certain ideas, facts and beliefs and hope that your brain kind of accepts them. Some people are probably easier to brainwash than others. And some people are naturally kinder or nastier or more elitist than others. Maybe the uploads are more in tune with the mindsets of the Hugos and Quentins of this world.'

'But you're so … independent,' I said blushing scarlet (and adding 'independent' instead of 'cool' or 'amazing' to try to look like less of a loved-up loser). 'An upload wouldn't change you.'

'My sister was pretty "independent",' Raf replied quietly. 'And they got to her.'

I nodded, unable to absorb everything he was saying. But what I still didn't get completely were Raf's demands for secrecy. I mean if Norms couldn't upload, why would it matter if one freakoid chose not to?

'Because it shows I don't trust the Ministry,' Raf explained. 'Through the TAA they're effectively weeding out the Norms.' I must have looked offended as Raf said, 'Sorry, 'weeding' was a bad choice of word but you know what I mean. Most young Norms are failing and as older Norms still in the Territory die, we're going to end up with a land filled with Childes. Who've all uploaded since they're nine. Who've all been brainwashed more or less into thinking the Ministry's great, that the TAA's fair, and that all they should do with their lives is work hard, obey the rules and help the Territory succeed. Basically they're creating model citizens.'

I stared at him in disbelief. Well, not disbelief, I totally believed everything he was saying, but in shock anyway.

'I mean you can understand it from their point of view – there'll be no crime, no one will join the Opposition. Everything will run really efficiently and if people just spend all their time working, they will probably discover cures and new energy sources quicker.'

I shuddered. I knew Jack and Daisy and I always joked about it, but to think they're making human robots – for real.

'If Childes started to choose not to upload, people would start to question everything. Their plans would fall apart. So that's why you can't tell anyone,' Raf repeated. 'Not even your mum or Daisy or Jack. No one.'

I nodded my agreement, knowing that nothing would ever make me betray this guy. Nothing in the world.

I've seen someone die. In real life. Not on the TV, but actually in front of me. We never watch the executions at home and even Mr Daniels isn't sick enough to make us watch them at school. Death happens more easily than I thought.

I was walking to school and had just turned our corner when I saw the protest up ahead on the other side of the road, outside some minor Ministry building. It wasn't much of a protest at that. Just four guys holding banners and chanting slogans. They weren't exactly hardened Opposition members as they didn't chant that loudly and you could tell they were properly scared from the way they jiggled nervously and kept looking round themselves all the time, as if they weren't even sure they really wanted the authorities to see their protest. I mean for real impact they should have been in the main square or outside a more major Ministry headquarters. But maybe this was the true face of the Opposition – a few scared people trying to stop what was wrong. Maybe a few was all it needed to kick others into action and start an unstoppable landslide.

The banners all had things like 'Ban the TAA' and 'Stop Killing our Children'. I knew I should have kept walking. Mum and Dad have always drilled it into me – survival rule number whatever: don't even look at any Opposition activity. Guilt by association and everything. But I couldn't seem to make my feet move away.

I recognised one of the men in the middle – Mr Patel. I guess Sunaina will be taking the TAA next year and he must feel her chances aren't great and he has to do something.

Minutes later a policeman turned the corner, saw the protestors and started to jog our way, unhooking his baton as he ran. Two of the protestors fled and Mr Patel was hesitating when I recognised the policeman's face. It was Marcus. Relief flooded me. I wanted to call out to Mr Patel to tell him to stand firm, that it was all going to be OK.

I smiled because it was like Mr Patel could hear my brain – he seemed to stand up straighter and his voice rose as Marcus covered the last few metres. 'Ban the TAA. Stop killing our children.'

That's when Marcus raised his baton. And then lowered it. A single sickening crunch and Mr Patel was lying in a pool of blood on the floor. He didn't scream or gasp out anything that showed that life had any meaning.

It was like turning off a light switch. The others ran. Marcus didn't bother to chase them. I guess it helps to have people spread the message about what happens to protestors. Makes the landslide pretty stoppable.

A police van pulled up and another policeman jumped out. The two of them dragged the body into the back of the van. As Marcus reversed into the van, our eyes met across the street and I swallowed in fear. What would he do to me? He must have seen that I'd stayed and watched and not pretended not to see as you're supposed to. Marcus waited for a car to pass then crossed the road towards me, maintaining eye contact the whole time.

He only started to speak when he was standing on the pavement directly in front of me.

'Sorry you had to see that,' he said, softly. 'You look upset?'

I sort of mumbled some combination of syllables.

'I know it looks brutal, love, but I'm just trying to keep these streets safe for you. Stop society from breaking down.'

I just swallowed and looked at the pavement, trying to make my bottom lip stop wobbling.

'I mean sometimes I think death is too good for these Opposition devils. Think about what they did to those babies. He'll be burning in hell right now, that's for sure.'

And then he gave me a normal friendly wink, gave my cheek a pinch and strode back to the van.

When you've grown up in a city seeing little more than the occasional rat and a couple of pigeons, a giraffe is pretty mind-blowing.

At breakfast Mum announced that she'd bought tickets to the zoo. I know this might seem like the lamest thing ever, but embarrassing as it is to admit it, I was actually pretty excited. She'd planned a 'proper family day out' saying that she was worried I was going to 'burn out early', but I think it's more likely that she was still feeling guilty about slapping me the other day. We don't exactly do family things really – there's always some emergency or other at Mum's work or I'm studying or Dad's working or, most commonly, all three. I hadn't been to the zoo since I was about eight, and remembered properly loving it then.

There used to be quite a few campaigns (shouty people with placards) to close the zoo based either on cruelty issues, as the cages are pretty small, or on the grounds that it was a 'waste of precious dry land'. But the scientists argued back that we needed to preserve as many species' genes as possible as we might need them in the future. Maybe they're planning to splice a bit of tiger DNA into mucor? Well, it wouldn't taste much worse if they did! Anyway, the scientists won (maybe because the shouty people were all massively annoyingly right on and ugly) and the zoo got to stay.

Anyway, typically, just after Mum's announcement, her emergency mobile rang and she was called out to some important case. Then the house phone rang and one of Dad's clients was about to be evicted so I was left Billy no mates with three tickets.

Mum urged me to take Daisy and Jack in their place. Said she thought it'd be 'nice for us to all be children for a day', at which I obviously did a massive eye roll. Dad told me not to roll my eyes at Mum and then got a bit concerned about my inviting Jack, but I reassured him for the millionth time that Jack's decking me was a one-off accident and not some new messed-up habit.

That said, I was stupidly a bit worried about spending the afternoon with Daisy and Jack. I knew I'd been a rubbish friend recently and had spent too much time with Raf. And things with Jack were still off and then there was the issue about the uploads that I couldn't speak about. I'd never kept secrets from Jack and Daisy before and felt pretty uncomfortable about starting now.

I shouldn't have worried though.

Despite it being a particularly lame day out, they both agreed to come immediately. Daisy responded with a, 'Hell, yeah!' but I think she'd be up for any break from studying. Jack too sounded amazingly keen and even apologised for being 'a bit of a denser recently'. This keenness faded a bit when I said Daisy was coming too, but then bounced right back up again when I confirmed that Raf wasn't.

We met at the zoo entrance, just off People's Park, and any weirdness between us vanished as soon as we stood in front of the first cage. There was a massive orangutan whose fur was basically identical to Jack's hair. It was hitting its fist on a tree stump and even Jack creased up as he accepted the resemblance. For the rest of the afternoon, Daisy and I would occasionally break mid-sentence to do an orangutan impression and we'd all be rolling about in hysterics.

We saw parrots and tigers and giraffes and lions and penguins and ate popcorn. Even the mucor burgers didn't seem to taste too bad.

The only time our moods dropped was when we reached the 'Territorial' section. Rather than your typical exotic 'zoo' animals, cage upon cage was filled with sheep, cows, pigs, chickens, rabbits. At one point I had to blink away tears as we stood in front of a tiny cage labelled: 'Dog'. Inside sat a sorry-looking spaniel, chained to a stump, tail low, its eyes brown pools of betrayal. A couple of toddlers pointed excitedly at it, as transfixed as they had been by the rhino and crocodile. Memories of Rex flooded back and Jack must have sensed them too as he came and wrapped me in a bear hug. For those few seconds I felt that no one else would ever understand me as well. I almost regretted Raf's coming to Hollets. Almost.

'How's it come to this?' I choked. 'Next, it's going to be one of us in a cage, chained to a stump, lump of mucor in a bowl, "Norm" written on the door.' I tried to laugh but it came out super hollow and we all shivered slightly at the same time.

'It might be better than the Wetlands,' Jack joked, trying to lift us out of our gloom. 'Sitting around all day being admired. Plenty of food. I think I'd be well suited to the role. Maybe I should campaign to be the first zoo Norm. What do you think?'

You know there are some days of your life you'll never forget, well this was one of them. Raf and I have just been on our first proper date and I've been grounded for, well, probably forever.

Raf snuck up behind me in the canteen while I was eating with Daisy and Jack and held two pieces of paper over my eyes. They were black and shiny.

'Guess what these are?' he whispered.

'The answers to today's History test?' I suggested, hopefully.

'Better,' he said, 'you of little imagination. So much better.'

Raf whisked his hands away and my eyes refocused to

see two tickets for Kaio's *Storm* concert. A stupidly big grin stretched across my face. These were hotter than anything imaginably hot. Kaio was only performing for one week this year and all the tickets had sold out within the first three milliseconds. Then I saw the date on the tickets.

'But they're for tonight,' I said glumly, knowing that there was no way that Mum was going to let me go out late on a Wednesday night with the TAA just over two weeks away.

'I'll cover for you,' Daisy offered. 'It'll be fine. You're always over at mine anyway. Say that I need you to help me revise. Your mum will believe that. I mean, anyone would believe that!' Daisy tried to sound light-hearted, but her fear came through and I felt like a really rubbish friend for not helping her more. But I really wanted to go. I really, really wanted to go.

'I'll leave you to your important discussions,' Jack broke in and then stormed off across the canteen. I thought he'd get better about this, about Raf, but looks like I was wrong.

'You should really go,' Daisy kept on.

'Please. Pretty please,' said Raf. And it was that, and his wolfish grin, and THOSE EYES that broke me.

'OK, OK, I'll call my mum. If you're sure, Daisy?' Daisy did over-exaggerated head nods and the next thing I knew I was calling my mum from the hall payphone and lying to her like I've never done before and never thought I'd ever do.

I was in such a state of excitement all afternoon that my pretty poor Geography test result just kind of passed me by and it took me a while to register why even Jack rubbed my arm and said not to worry, that it'd be OK. I know I've got to get a grip, particularly with my two point deduction, but I told myself that that grip's going to start tomorrow.

After school, I went straight to Daisy's to borrow some clothes and basically make my story more convincing. Daisy's parents weren't even there, as per usual. I reached into Daisy's cupboard to pull out a pair of her jeans, we're basically the same size, but Daisy dragged me out immediately.

'You're going on a date.' Daisy spelt out as if I were a complete denser. 'You're not wearing my old jeans on a date.'

The next twenty minutes were pretty horrific. Daisy forced me into a number of different outfits, all more revealing than the last, and I felt like I'd somehow descended into makeover hell.

At last she declared herself happy. I was squeezed into a tiny black skirt and a black top with gold sequins on the shoulder and slashes across the back.

'I look like I've got gold dandruff and have been savaged by a tiger.'

Daisy pouted. I don't think this was the praise she'd been looking for.

The doorbell rang.

'Have an amazing night.' Daisy hugged me and I opened the door to Raf's grinning face. He held the door open and as I walked under his arm he stroked his hand across the back of my top and made a 'grrrr' sound. I recoiled in embarrassment.

'I know, I look ridiculous,' I said as we got on the bus.

'You don't look ridiculous. You do look a bit too much like Daisy. But you look beautiful. As always. You'd even look beautiful if you'd been clawed by an actual cat rather than a pair of scissors.' And then he put his arm round me and I sort of nuzzled in.

The concert was mad when we got there. There were so many people. All our sort of age. People crammed in together so close that you couldn't tell who was a Norm and who was a freakoid and there was this crazy atmosphere like everyone needed to party as no one, especially the Norms, knew what the future, if they even had one, held. Massive spotlights lit the stadium and the speakers were as high as cliffs. There were loads of police, probably to protect Kaio from his hordes of female fans, and cameras everywhere, ready to catch the poster boy doing his stuff live. When the cameras swivelled in our direction, I shrank away and Raf laughed.

'Do you really think your parents are going to be

watching this?' I laughed too at the absurdity of the idea. My mum dancing (or as she cringeworthily says, 'bopping') away to Kaio as she does the ironing.

When Kaio came on stage, the whole stadium sort of erupted. His first song was *Into the Dark* and everyone's playing it on their Scribe at the moment so you can imagine what reaction that caused. Huge pillars of red and gold light were projected up on either side of the stage and there must have been at least fifty dancers on stage with Kaio, mirroring his movements exactly. The whole effect was incredible, sinister too, but in a really cool way. When he finished, the whole stadium was vibrating to chants of, 'Kaio, Kaio'. The next two songs were from an earlier download and just blew the roof off as well.

But it was the fourth song that changed everything. Kaio doesn't normally introduce his songs. He might say this one's for blah-de-blah, but not much more than that. But this time he waited until the whole stadium was quiet and then looked all serious; almost unrecognisable as he's normally always got this hot grin on. 'This next one's a new song,' he began. 'It's for everyone out there doing their TAA this year. It's for everyone who's lost someone. It's for everyone who thinks this system stinks. Which it does. I know I'm partly to blame as I've supported it. But that stops here. That stops tonight. So here goes. This is my new song – *The Line*. Hope you enjoy it.'

The next few minutes seemed to happen in suspended

time. The drummer started the beat and then Kaio began
to sing:

You say good luck and stay dry
As they line up like cattle to die
Just plug in your Node
Information overload
Don't listen as the little ones cry

Half the audience, still as waxworks, watched Kaio. The
other half, including me and Raf, watched the police. At
first they seemed like robots about to malfunction, jerking
this way and that, looking for leadership. Clearly no one
had expected this. Kaio was the Ministry's darling after
all. Then suddenly it was as if a switch had been flicked
and the police came to life. They began to storm the
stage. Arms flailed, the drummer was knocked over and a
policeman had Kaio in a headlock on the ground. Police
started to stream into the stadium and you could taste the
fear in the air as everyone turned to run. Raf grabbed my
hand and pulled me along beside him. We clambered
through and round people, pushing, clutching, running.
At one point a couple in front of us tripped and fell and
we didn't stop, we just ran over them, survival was
everything. Anyone caught from the concert would be
marked as a potential Subversive.

We managed to crawl under a metal seat at the back of

the stadium and through a hole in the wire mesh fence. The wire claimed half of Daisy's skirt and tore into my right leg. The next thing I knew Raf had grabbed my hand again and I was running, warm blood trickling down my calf. We knew we had to make it home on foot, that the police would already be stopping and searching the busses. We decided the safest route was probably through People's Park as there were fewer CCTVs there, so we clambered over the railings and began following the stream to the south end. Just when we thought we'd left all the police behind us, the night was sliced open by a high intensity torch beam. We both dived to the ground, tasting mud as our heads hit the path. Lights and voices shot overhead. My ears were filled with the sound of my heart thudding and all I could think was, 'They've found us, they've found us.'

A radio crackled. A deep voice answered. 'Negative.' Then the voices and the lights receded.

Raf walked his fingers along the path to interlock with mine and we lay there for some time, bathing in relief. I finally rolled onto my back and spat the mud out of my mouth. The taste lingered.

Above, myriads of stars seemed to mock us.

We made the rest of our way back in silence. Words would have seemed trite and the clasp of Raf's hand brought comfort enough. I finally stumbled through my front door just after 3am. My mum was sitting on the sofa, a single desk lamp illuminating her blank expression, red eyes and very straight back.

The TV was paused on the news channel. There, freeze-frame, was the concert with police with their raised batons and teenagers running. In the bottom of the left of the frame you could just make out mine and Raf's faces.

'They arrested one hundred and twenty-four teenagers,' Mum said quietly. 'One hundred and twenty-four.'

'I'm so sorry, Mum.' I said, bursting into tears. 'I had no idea, no one had any idea ... I just really wanted to go.'

'I'd have let you, you know. Go, that is. I just want you to be safe. I love you so much.' And then she started crying too and I wished she'd just got angry with me as this made me feel so much worse.

'No more secrets from now on,' Mum said.

'No more secrets,' I agreed.

'And you're grounded.'

Today was a *Newsflash!* day. You know, the sort of day when they interrupt all channels to broadcast some massively important news and everyone speaks in exclamation marks. Dad and I were trying to watch a comedy set in space. It's pretty lame but we watch it together every Tuesday evening. It's our father-daughter thing and a half-hour liferaft in a sea of revision. Dad even makes popcorn and we moan about what stereotypes we've become, but we both secretly love it. Each episode ends with Astronaut Tyrone staring into the camera and saying, 'One week to go and counting.' We always both join in and Dad does the worst impression you've ever heard. Accents really aren't his thing.

Tonight was going to be extra special as Mum and Dad have just ungrounded me. Apparently they'd had this really long discussion and decided that everyone makes mistakes when they're young and that it's OK as long as you learn from them and don't mess up again in the same way. The real issue they said was that I'd lied to them about where I was so I'm allowed out as long as I'm totally honest, and it's to Daisy's, Jack's or possibly Raf's (yet to be decided!), and it's to study, and I'm back by 9pm.

But we didn't get to watch Astronaut Tyrone's semi-tragic mishaps after all because they've finally caught Archie Rycroft. Yes, the unbelievably dumb Archie Rycroft who's been on the run for eleven months. The Archie Rycroft who managed to be the first freakoid to fail the TAA in three years. More used to fail at the start. Before the exam format changed. Before, I guess, loads of Ministers had freakoid children themselves. When Archie failed, people didn't talk about anything else for two weeks. It wasn't in the paper or in the Bulletins of course, but word spread and everyone in the First City seemed to have heard somehow or other. Lots of freakoid parents started going a bit crazy as they suddenly realised that they'd spent all this money but still hadn't necessarily bought a nice dry place for their beloved sprog. Sending excess children to die in the Wetlands suddenly looked less totally good. Someone high up in the Ministry pushed through more changes to the exam format. More recall, fewer essays. Dad thinks he heard somewhere that that guy had a son in my year.

When the police turned up on Results Day, young Archie was long gone. His parents were sitting calmly in their huge mansion but Archie's bed was bare. Norms try to disappear every Results Day. Of course they do. Why else would they have brought in the prison-like Waiting Places, which makes it way harder? But Norms are always caught. Quickly. And then shipped off. As punishment they're not even given a basic survival kit. No iodine. No mosquito net. And if they run before the results are published, they're shipped off even if they've actually passed.

But Archie Rycroft, of the massively rich and important and definitely inbred Rycrofts, miraculously avoided capture. And he was clearly not doing some massively cunning manoeuvres. Judging by his TAA score, there really aren't many humans he could outwit. Possibly a leftover Neanderthal. Or the victim of a botched late upgrade. And everyone knew the police weren't really looking that hard. I mean his parents weren't even arrested.

This obviously made loads of Norms cross. And I mean riot cross. There were serious clashes between protestors and police.

That was back in July last year. Now eleven months later, they've found him. The policewoman being interviewed claimed that Archie had been living in a hole in the Arable Lands. Surviving off crops and insects. But he didn't look that dirty. Or that thin. I mean he still had this gross little pot belly peeping out from under his t-shirt.

And then the presenter made the real game-changing announcement. From this year, freakoids as well as Norms would have to go to a Waiting Place to sit the exam and wait for results.

I laughed aloud as I imagined Hugo's reaction. Ha ha – pack your bag like the rest of us! Dad didn't join in. He just looked super-serious.

'Interesting,' he said. 'I wonder what this is leading to. This is the first time they've even openly acknowledged that Archie Rycroft was on the run.' He had his worried look on. His eyebrows always skulk together when he's worried.

He can also be slightly paranoid.

'Maybe there've been more riots,' I said. 'Maybe they knew they needed to find him this time and look like they were equalising things a bit. Before they ship the next lot of us Norms out.'

'No one's shipping you anywhere, baby.' He tried to sound reassuring, but his eyebrows kept on skulking.

Just when I thought things might be on their way back to normal with Jack, this happens and I lose him again. I think he might even hate me a bit. All his anger, and I totally get this anger, has been funnelled into one massive blame plaster and stuck on my head.

After the initial announcement in Assembly, he avoided me in Physics and Geography and then when I tried to speak to him at lunch he had so much stress in his face that it actually turned it ugly – like one of those gargoyles you see on the oldest churches.

But it's not like I knew what was going to happen at that concert, not like I knew that Kaio was going to go all off-script and Oppositiony. And normally Jack would have been in favour of anyone mouthing off against the Ministry anyway. It's just that this time the consequences were so awful and so relevant.

At 7am this morning, the Ministry decided to abolish the SAM programme. Mr Daniels showed us the official video of the announcement. A guy who looked like he had an unhealthy amount of rat DNA in him stared into the camera. He wore a grey striped suit and over-ironed shirt and spoke in a voice that hundreds of little image consultants had clearly decided struck exactly the right balance between sternly authoritative and grandfatherly reassuring.

'The highly regrettable events of last week's concert,' he began, my heart already in my mouth, 'have led the Ministry to the unfortunate but inevitable conclusion that the cultivation and elevation of artistic and literary talent at the expense of the solid skills of scientific reason and critical thinking has allowed a dissident element to emerge in our society.'

Daisy and I looked at each other. She mimed incomprehension as she's not great with three syllable words at the best of times, but a knot was already forming in my stomach. I knew where this was going.

'The destabilising and terrorist-sponsored actions of first Frankie Lebore and now Kaio have shown that, as scientists have long thought, an over-active right-brain is frequently linked to an unstable and unsound mind. To this end, the Ministry, after consultation with leading figures in education and the High Priest, has decided to abolish the SAM programme and require all young citizens to obtain a minimum 70 per cent in this year's TAA. As the detention and resettlement of Archie Rycroft and the universal application of the Waiting Place scheme has demonstrated, the examination system is fair and impartial, applying equally to all candidates, regardless of colour, class or creed. No special treatment is given to Childes and likewise no dispensation should be awarded to non-upgraded individuals on any basis. Thank you.' And with a crackle, the rat man was gone.

Dad wasn't being paranoid. Producing Archie Rycroft had just been part of the game. He was a pawn like the rest of us. I almost felt sorry for him. But I didn't have time for that. All my thoughts were with Jack. This meant it was all wasted. All that time Jack had spent drawing, sketching, planning: wasted. Time he could have spent revising: gone. I just wanted to wrap my arms round him and tell him that I'd help, that I'd coach him, that I'd never let anything bad happen to my best friend. But he was already out of reach.

And what was really annoying, not that annoying is a strong-enough word, is that when the rat said, 'leading figures in education,' Mr Daniels' chest puffed up all proud-looking, boasting about his involvement. Well done headmaster, that's another life you've put at risk. You must be really proud. In it for the kids.

So do you want the good news or the bad news? Dad always says give the good news first and then sting them with the bad (or in his case, the bill) later.

The good news:

1) So far, touch wood, no policemen have turned up at home or at school looking for me or Raf so it seems they can't be hunting down people from the TV footage of the Kaio concert. First thing this morning at school I saw a guy in a suit I'd never seen before loitering in the Maths block and I started having heart palpitations, but then someone said he was from the computer company and was there to mend a Port.

2) Jack seems to have finally gotten round to forgiving me. I accidentally on purpose tripped Hugo over during football and he made such a piteous yelp as he fell that I couldn't help laughing and Jack, momentarily forgetting that he was mad at me, ran up and gave me a high five. He then remembered that he was supposed to hate me and looked confused for a bit, before giving in to the forgiveness vibe. I'm so pleased. Jack's been around forever and it's like my axis is knocked without him. I'm going to study with him every other day now until the exams. I could tell Mum and Dad were really torn when I told them this. I mean they totally trust that I'll study and everything when I'm with him. With two weeks to go I'd have to be a total denser not to. They love Jack like he's their own. And they know that he's much more likely to pass with my help. But they also know that I'd cover the stuff more quickly if I were by myself.

3) Uncle Pete isn't coming to stay after all. He's got to

give some very important lectures (yeah, right) so we'll have to cope without his horrific presence for a few more months.

4) Amanda still wasn't back at school today. That makes nearly two weeks she's been off. It also meant I could sit through double maths without having to watch her drool all over Hugo. Once, I swear I actually saw a bit of saliva drop out of her open mouth. Super grim. Tom Williams has started taking bets on what's up. The options so far are:

- She's got a really bad spot
- She's pregnant
- She's got some hideous infectious disease.

I put one Gold on option two but I'm crossing my fingers for option three! It would totally serve her right if she got something like leprosy and her nose fell off. It's so unfair though. There's no way a Norm could ever take this much time off this close to the exam, no matter how ill they were. I guess she'll just upload some catch-up program and shake-shake-shake-eye roll – there you go.

The bad news:

Daisy's been grounded now! Talk about malcy. And it's until the end of the exams! Her mum found her results card for the recent tests in her bag and threw an epi fit. She then had to go and lie down from a migraine, decided to do this on a sofa in the lounge, moved the sofa so it was further from the light and uncovered the bloodstain on the wallpaper from Daisy's party. That's when she decided to ruin Daisy's life. I'm not even allowed to go round there. Apparently I'm not such a great influence after all. Now Daisy's got a tutor every evening and we'll only get to talk at break. Her tutor's called Gil and according to Daisy he's a total neek. He's got bad acne even though he's probably about twenty-one and greasy, limp hair with visible flakes of dandruff. Even grimmer, he's got a spindly neck with a massive Adam's apple so he looks like he's swallowed a ping-pong ball. She says he does this lame swallow every time before he speaks which makes his Adam's apple bob up and down as he does a 'gugh' noise. Her mum's so stupid. If she'd got Daisy a hot tutor, she'd do loads better, just to impress him.

I think Daisy's getting properly scared by the exams too. She's losing weight. She's always been thin, but now she's got hollows under her eyes and her cheekbones jut out even more than before. She's talking about the Wetlands as if she's going to be sent there. Which she can't be. I won't let it happen. But she says she's running out of options.

Mum's been acting really weirdly recently as well. Tonight, when she was putting on the washing, I told her about Amanda still not being at school and she came out with, 'Maybe her parents have been transferred somewhere like the Fourth City and she's had to change schools.' I laughed, assuming that Mum was being freakily specific as a joke. Mum can have a weird sense of

129

humour. I think it's being a scientist. Most of the people she works with are similarly socially inept. But this time Mum joined in laughing a split second too late and just seemed to burrow deeper into the washing machine.

I never thought it was possible to work this hard. Today I've done nine hours at school. Sport's gone. It's now extra Maths. Lunch hour has been cut to twenty minutes. First break's gone.

Then after school it was straight to Jack's for another three hours of science.

And I hardly slept last night. Scientific fact: too much cortisol (that's stress hormone) in your system can cause insomnia. Not exactly what I need at the moment.

But not sleeping's sometimes better than actually sleeping. No nightmares. They're getting more and more vivid, the nightmares I mean. In the most frequent one, I'm sitting down to eat at our table, but it's just me by myself. I'm vaguely aware that Mum and Dad are somewhere, but I can't see or hear them. And there are flies everywhere. And they're biting me again and again. I look at my plate and the mucor morphs into this enormous fish that then turns and looks up at me, and it's got my face.

I guess I'm trying to blame it all on work, on stress, but maybe I'm just a properly rubbish friend and a selfish pain.

Something just seemed to flip in my head when Jack didn't get the Force and Motion section of Physics for the third time. I couldn't help it. An exasperated, 'Aaaaggghhhh!' burst out of me and I said, 'Come on, Jack, you're killing me.' And then there was just the worst, the loudest silence ever.

All I'd meant was that he was stressing me out, but he took my words literally and started pacing around the room, clenching and unclenching his fists. I was worried he might hit me or something, but then the anger seemed to fizzle out inside him and he went all quiet. When he finally spoke, he said maybe it'd be best for me to study by myself as he was dragging me down. That I needed to focus with my two point deduction. That he'd never forgive himself if he was the reason that I failed and got sent to die.

And I tried to talk him round. I cracked rubbish jokes. I even did a stupid dance for him. And big baby eyes. But nothing worked. He was adamant. 'I've loved you forever, Noa,' he said.

I blushed, wanting to put my hands over my ears, block out the one conversation that I didn't want to have. But he seemed to read my mind and stood close, pinning my hands to my waist and forcing me to look him in the eye.

'No more jokes, Noa. Not now. Just listen. I love you. I

loved you when we were six and playing with Rex. I loved you when we were ten and doing running races in People's Park. I loved you when we were twelve and learning how to make ourselves faint by holding our breath too long. I've loved you every day of my useless life and I'm not going to be the one who kills you.'

I don't know what the right way to react would have been but I'm pretty sure I didn't do it. All I could think was, This is so horrifically awkward, run away! and that's basically what I did. I said I had to get home, that this wasn't the time, and scurried off, away from the look of hurt in Jack's eyes.

I'd always sort of known this day would come. That there was and always had been this thing between us. I'd always thought that when we did have THE conversation, that thing would have built and built and we'd sort of end up together and it'd be the sort of relationship which is even more amazing because you'd been friends first. But why now? Why when we're sitting exams in days? Why when I've met Raf and have completely fallen for him?

I closed my eyes and tried to imagine kissing Jack. Burrowing into his arms. But even in my imagination, his arms morph into Raf's arms and his lips into Raf's lips.

'Class-time' always means trouble.

We had a non-timetabled Class-time session with Ms Jones so were ten minutes late for Geography. Normally a bonus. Geography is such a pointless subject. Just one step below RS. At least there's no RS in Year 10. There's no RS section in the TAA, although Dad says with the Archbishop gaining more and more influence that might change. But, not meaning to sound totally selfish and everything, it doesn't affect me so right now I really don't care.

Anyway, Ms Jones gathered us all round with a fake look of concern on her evil, reptilian face. I sat next to Jack and tried to smile at him in a 'look, everything's still cool between us' kind of way, but he refused to look at me. Ms Jones told us that Amanda Marsden wouldn't be returning to Hollets. That Amanda had asked Ms Jones to say goodbye to her classmates on her behalf and to wish us well in the TAA. Yeah, right. Like they were close. Everyone looked a bit suspicious. This was not the Amanda we all knew and didn't love. Did she ask Ms Jones to snog Hugo goodbye for her? That'd be more her style. People do leave all the time as there aren't that many good jobs going so if your mum or dad get transferred, off go all the family, you don't really get a choice in the matter.

But everyone always says goodbye themselves and teachers never make a big deal about it. And no one leaves two weeks, sorry thirteen days, before the TAA.

'Where's she gone?' David asked.

Ms Jones replied, 'Her father's been transferred. It's a very high profile hush-hush position so I'd be grateful if you don't discuss it too much with your families.'

'But where?' Seems like Amanda should have gone for David instead of Hugo. He's persistent at least while Hugo was just staring at his hands. I think he was actually comparing the sizes of his thumbs. Honest to God. Freakoid.

Ms Jones fixed dead-fish eyes on David. 'They've moved to the Fourth City.'

I thought I knew Mum. I thought I knew her as well as it's possible to know another person. Turns out I was wrong.

School was cancelled today. Now this was something big. School is never cancelled. And this close to the TAA. No way. Heavy snow, heatwaves, freak sandstorms, you name it, we have to trudge to the gates of Hollets hell and freeze/bake/get sanded raw regardless. But today was different. Mum got a phone call from Sam Neville's mum (through the school's lame 'snowball' emergency call system) saying the school was shut due to a bomb scare. I wonder who would want to blow up Hollets? I mean I know loads of people who hate it, but they're all fifteen and don't exactly own huge supplies of explosives. I'm surprised if we've somehow got on to the Opposition's radar.

The phone call came during breakfast. Dad actually looked up from his toast and paper to ask what was going on. And that is remarkable – Dad's not a good morning person. He looks a bit like a mole first thing. Squinty eyes, glasses on, big curly hair not yet tamed into lawyer style. To be fair I look pretty much the same. Thanks Dad for those great genes!

'I thought catching Archie Rycroft was going to stop this sort of thing,' he mumbled through toast crumbs.

'I guess they're showing that it's not enough,' Mum replied. 'Or maybe it's because they abolished the SAMs.'

I wasn't too stressed about it. We've basically finished the syllabus in nearly every subject and I could revise just as well at home as at school. I've never been one of those find-it-hard-to-concentrate people. In fact I go into super-concentration overdrive. Once, when I was studying with Daisy, she had to hit me over the head with a magazine before I realised she was talking to me. She'd tried yelling at me a few times first and I literally couldn't hear her; I'd just blocked out any noise. Apparently that's why I do well in exams.

Mum told me to hurry up and get dressed. I asked what all the fuss was about. After all, I could just study in my room in my pyjamas.

But Mum had different plans. I had to go to her work with her. Said if there were bomb threats the Opposition might be out to generally cause trouble. That there might be riots or street fights. My moaning was ignored and five minutes later I was dressed and out of the flat. Mum nearly didn't even let me stop to put my contact lenses in, but there was NO WAY I was going anywhere near people in my glasses, especially as, if I was having to go with Mum to the Laboratory, it was massively likely that Raf might be going there too with his dad.

When we got to the Laboratory we had to go through the endless security: bag search, body scanners, fingerprint identification. I even had to have my photo taken for a temporary clearance pass. I blinked in the flash so my eyes were half closed in the photo and I looked like a right denser. Great that I had to have that pinned to my top all day.

Mum's office was on the fifth floor (the lift labelled the floor 'Disease Prevention'). It was the first time I'd been there since I was seven and had to stay off school for four days with tonsillitis. The door was marked 'Dr R Blake: Senior Scientist' and I felt really proud. This was before I knew.

Her desk was cluttered. There was a large computer screen, several other flashing displays, a phone and lots of photos of me and Dad. I'm sure there used to be one of her pregnant, with Dad's arms wrapped round her swollen belly. But if so, that's gone now. I guess nearly everyone who works for the Ministry uses a Wombpod so photos of big bellies are sort of frowned on.

Down the corridor, leading away from the lift, were loads of airlocks and I could just about make out some scientists wearing some bad-ass spacesuits. I remember thinking this is way cooler than school science. Take that, Group 1 metals! Mr Malovich would be way out of his depth here!

Mum said I had to sit in her office and revise there. That it was too dangerous for me to go down the corridor. Really dangerous. I might disrupt some major experiment or get exposed to horrific germs.

'Do you promise me, Noa?' she asked, all serious with extreme eye contact.

I nodded.

And I meant to keep my promise, I really did.

Just before lunchtime I was about to literally die from boredom. I hadn't moved for four hours and my eyes were semi-glazed from focusing on my Scribe for that long. I needed to move to get rid of the pins and needles in my feet and the random cramp in my left calf. Typically I was in the middle of some well-embarrassing star jumps when Raf put his head round the door.

'Company?' he asked, starting to star jump in time next to me.

'How did you know where I'd be?' I asked, laughing.

He explained that he'd looked at the floor plan.

'There's only one Dr Blake here,' he said, eyes all twinkling.

I felt like a denser.

He looked at my top. 'Nice photo,' he joked.

I felt like even more of a denser.

Time passed a lot faster with Raf there. He slung his right arm around my shoulder and we just sort of snuggled into the sofa, Scribes on our laps. We made a deal to revise for forty-five mins then chat/whatever for fifteen mins and keep alternating. We'd got through the first two sections of Chemistry when one of the monitors on Mum's desk started beeping furiously. And the red 'emergency' light on it was flashing.

'Looks important, shall we get your mum?' Raf asked.

I was torn. I know I'd promised to stay put but this did seem massively important. And there was no one else around. No scientists in the corridor. Even the spacesuits had gone.

'Come on,' Raf urged. 'I don't know about you, but aren't you at least a little curious to find out what they do down there? My dad doesn't tell me anything.'

I gave in. Raf was right – I was curious. I knew nothing really about Mum's work. Just that she worked on cures. Was paid by the Ministry. Was one of the good guys.

We didn't want to catch any super-evil-bug so we put

on facemasks that were hanging off the back of Mum's door. Raf managed to operate the first airlock. There was a red lever you had to push in and twist clockwise at the same time. A bit like a safety cap on a bottle of medicine. The door opened and shut again with a horrible gulp of air. Like we were being swallowed and then spat out again by a huge fish.

It was very quiet on the other side of the airlock. I called Mum's name and the sound seemed to bounce off the walls. The corridor narrowed and there were lots of tiny rooms off it that you could look into through circular windows at head height. The first two rooms were filled with cages of rats. White rats with pink eyes. Some seemed healthy. Others lay twitching, covered in pustules.

But it was the third room that changed everything. It was much larger than the first two rooms. We peered through the glass and saw three single beds, each covered in a clear tent with all these tubes in it. On each bed lay a teenager, a drip in their left arm. Covered in pustules. Twitching. And I recognised them all.

Lying on the beds nearest the windows and labelled 'Subject 64' and 'Subject 65' were Neil Hurst and Rosie Hood. They'd been a year above me at Hollets. Both Norms. Both had failed their TAA and everyone thought they'd been shipped off to the Wetlands. I remember them particularly as we'd all felt so sorry for them 'cos their parents had opted to stay. On the bed by the door, labelled 'Case 42 – Immuno-Deficiency-Virus' lay Amanda.

We watched, paralysed, as a nurse in a starched white uniform used a syringe to extract a sample of blood from one of the tubes attached to Amanda and then inject it into the tubes attached to Neil and Rosie. She then opened and injected a vial of purple liquid into a separate tube attached to Neil. A computer screen flashed rapidly increasing numbers and Neil's chest started to heave up and down.

The nurse then turned to leave. She was about to look through the door window. Straight at us.

'Come on,' Raf hissed into my ear. 'We've got to get out of here. Now.' I could hardly breathe. I sprinted back along the corridor, Raf behind me. We opened the airlock again and I ran into the bathroom and puked again and again until I was just heaving up this yellow rancid bile.

When I walked, zombie-like, back into Mum's office, she was there filing some papers.

'Noa, where have you been?' she demanded. 'I just asked you to do one simple thing – to stay put. I need to be able to trust you.'

I did a sort of cough/seal-bark laugh. Trust. The hypocrisy. 'There was an emergency so I went to get you, Mum. I went down the corridor to get you.' My words were like ice and as our eyes met, I could see fear in hers.

I look about two hundred years old, my eyes are so swollen from crying, but I finally feel a bit better. Some of the ancient cultures that were all about energy rather than medicine and blood and stuff thought crying releases bad, built-up energy and maybe that's not complete rubbish after all.

Mum and I didn't talk after the Laboratory. We just sat in silence in the car on the way home and it was so tense, like there was this massive pressure in the car, like when you change height suddenly and your eardrums go all weird and then pop.

When Dad got home, Mum dragged him into their room and I could hear them have this secretive conversation. All I could make out was:

Dad: 'Oh God, so she knows. What have you told her?'

Mum: 'Oh God. Nothing. She saw Amanda. Oh God.'

So that cleared something up at least. Dad's a bad guy too. The popcorn-making, daughter-cuddling, Astronaut Tyrone-watching father doubles as an evil child-experimenter-on approver.

At 7pm, when we normally sit down to dinner, Mum and Dad re-emerged from their room and said, at the exact same time, 'Noa-bean, we need to talk.'

I flinched at that. How could they think it was OK to

use that name? Is 'use a term of endearment' listed on page twenty-nine of the official guide to being horrific phoney parents who pretend to be really good but actually kill kids?

Mum spoke first. She said she'd started to work at the Laboratory in 2029. She was twenty-three and had just met Dad. She'd just finished university, topping her year in Biochemistry, and the Ministry had only just come to power. The Dark Days were nearly over but the Fence hadn't been built yet.

I sort of sniff-coughed at the mention of the Dark Days. Mr Daniels and other phoneys are always going on about them, but how exactly could things be much worse than now? More Ministry lies.

Dad clearly noticed my reaction and said, 'Seriously Noa, they really were bad times. People, good, normal people, were murdered every day. Stabbed in the street, killed in their homes. Everyone was desperate — there simply wasn't enough to go round.'

'How many people did you kill then, Mum?' I asked, all mock sweetness. No reply. Just a look of phoney shock. 'Oh, the murdering started later, did it, Mum? Sorry, experimenting, isn't it. Sciencey murdering.'

Dad did a funny sort of twitch but kept looking me straight in the eye. 'You have no idea, Noa. People were being killed for the smallest things. Food, medicine, land. Land was everything. My older brother, Max...' Dad stopped speaking and looked like he was silently choking. He then pulled himself together and continued. 'Max was hung and nailed to a fence as a warning by a gang who took his house because it was on slightly higher land. He'd refused to hand it over to them. Even when they turned up with clubs and knives. I was the one who found and took down his body.'

Oh God. I swallowed. No wonder Dad had never wanted to talk about him. A tear slid down Dad's cheek. I think that's the first time I've ever seen him cry.

I closed my mouth and Mum took a deep breath, all Daisy's-mum's-yoga-video like, and kept on speaking.

The Laboratory job was a research role, looking for cures for the new, particularly horrible diseases that were infecting people in the flooded areas. The medicines produced were going to be handed out for free.

'So you're a saint then, are you, Mum?'

'Noa, please, Noa, just let me try and explain. Will you do that?' Her red eyes were so pitiful, I nodded and let her continue.

Mum rose up the department quickly. Then changes began. The Fence was built and the Territory came into being. The TAA was introduced and the Childe procedure was invented and patented. Mum and Dad were against these changes, but believed that overall Mum was doing good so should keep working there. And the Dark Days had been so bad. 'It's not all black and white, Noa. Life's more complicated than that. Before the Fence, no one had the chance of a good life.'

'Limited space requires limited numbers,' I quoted at them in monotone. 'And the changes didn't affect you, did they?' I added. I think that hit home as they both looked away from me as I said it.

Then I was born and the job, because it was a Ministry position, had its benefits. They could have had a freakoid for free if they'd wanted to, and even though they'd chosen not to, they still got free schooling at Hollets for me, which they'd never otherwise have been able to afford, not in a million years.

'And the experiments,' I persisted, there was no way I was going to let Mum duck this. 'When did they start?'

Big pause. She was clearly deciding whether she could get away with a lie and realised she couldn't, that I'd just know she was 100 per cent evil and not to be trusted and that would really be it for us.

'Five years ago,' Mum replied numbly.

'Five years!' I exploded. 'You've been killing kids for five years!'

Mum's back straightened and although her voice was now trembling, she kept on talking. Five years ago their role changed. 'Prioritisation' was the word from the top. Medicine was no longer going to be made available to the Wetlands. All funds would be concentrated on stopping diseases reaching the Territory and curing any infection that did breach the border. To that end, human experimentation was introduced to speed up tests for potential cures. Children who'd failed the TAA and were going to be sent unaccompanied to the Wetlands were chosen as the best available test subjects as their chances of survival were next to nothing anyway.

And, more to the point, no one would miss them.

'Your mum has saved lives too, Noa. With the cures she's found. She's helped children too.'

'Dad, just stay out of this now, OK?' I shouted. 'What about your whole lawyer spiel you're always going on about – it's more important to save the innocent than, well, than anything! So why didn't you quit, Mum? That's what I don't understand.' By now I was sobbing. 'When you were asked to do this, why didn't you just quit?'

'Because of you,' Mum sobbed back. 'Because if I lost my job, you'd be taken out of Hollets and we'd be in the same position as Aunty Vicki and Ella. You wouldn't stand a chance of passing the TAA. And from the first minute I held you in my arms I knew I'd kill for you. I just didn't think I'd have to.' And then the floodgates really opened and it was like I could see into her soul and see all the guilt and the love and the fierce protection just flowing out of her.

'Sorry, Mum,' I choked. 'I love you, Mum.'

'I love you too, Noa-bean.'

Raf was waiting for me as arranged outside the front entrance to school. He was wearing a pair of sunglasses even though it wasn't remotely sunny. He wrapped his arms around me tighter and tighter, only stopping when my ribs made a funny sort of cracking sound. He then traced his finger gently round my eyes. Great, the five layers of foundation obviously failed to cover up my humungo puffy bags. Standing on tiptoes, I reached up and pulled the sunglasses from his face and then drew back in shock.

Round his green eye was a massive blue-green bruise. It was really disturbing as it was almost beautiful in a way, as all the colours sort of complemented each other, but also really ugly, like some weird painting Jack might draw.

'What happened?' I asked anxiously.

'My dad wasn't too happy when he heard about our adventure at the Laboratory.' Raf tried to sound all sarky and relaxed like normal, but it didn't work. The pain shone through.

He paused for a moment and then decided to drop the jokey act. 'Noa, we're better off without them. My dad, your mum, they're not good people. At least we know that now.'

'But they only did what they had to, to protect us. So that we could stay at Hollets and pass the TAA.'

Raf's eyes blinked and his whole face seemed to go in and out of focus. Then the saddest smile spread across his face.

'What?' I asked. 'What did I say?'

'Don't worry, Noa. I guess I just wanted our parents to be alike. If they were both bad, then they wouldn't be as bad, what they did wouldn't be as bad, do you see?' I did kind of understand his twisted logic.

'But I still don't get it,' I continued like a moron, 'your dad was probably doing it for you too.'

'Noa,' Raf spoke gently, as if I were some denser baby. 'You and I might like to forget it and pretend it's not true, but I'm a *freakoid*. I could go to any school, upload the information and pass the TAA. My dad doesn't know I don't upload. He didn't do this for me. He did it for him. For the status. For the money. And I think he's fine about that. Come on, I mean he took the job there a month ago, after they'd been doing this for years! He could easily have stayed at his old job if he'd wanted to. He was originally a mechanical engineer before he went into medicine. He could have designed robots for the refuse centre. He could have designed robots to look after old people. He just didn't.'

I couldn't think of anything to say so this time I put my arms round him and squeezed. He smelt of burnt leaves.

'For what it's worth, I'm pleased he moved jobs.' I said and then cringed. A month ago I could never have imagined I'd turn into such a cheesemonger. And the worst bit is that whenever I try and say something real or sincere, my voice does this sort of spasm and I end up sounding massively insincere and a real phoney denser.

Raf laughed despite himself. 'Wow, that sounded sarcastic.'

'I'm sorry. It wasn't meant to.'

'I got that. I know you pretty well now, Noa Blake. Your complete inability to sound sincere is one of the many things I love about you.'

Yes, he said love. And THAT word hung in the air like a little bubble between us. I didn't know what to say, I just sort of stared past his face and focused on his right ear, as that seemed safely neutral. I couldn't quite bear to look into his eyes as I felt it'd be just too intense and I might drown or spontaneously combust or something.

But what I really wanted to say was, 'I love you too. So so much. And I'm so pleased your dad decided to move jobs and come and experiment on children because otherwise I'd never have met you and my life would be far worse.' But I didn't, of course. I said nothing and then the bell rang and the bubble burst.

'What are you going to do?' I asked as we headed up the main steps.

'Nothing,' Raf replied, 'for now.'

'And later?'

'I'm going to bring this whole system down.' And he spoke with such grim determination that I believed him.

Sometimes peace offerings come in circle-shaped boxes.

Raf walked me home after school. I'd wanted to spend the evening revising with him. Things are so awkward with Jack now that he doesn't want my help any more. But Dad said at breakfast that he wanted me at home this evening. That he wasn't getting enough time with his little girl. He was trying to sound all casual about it, because he didn't exactly want to say, 'In case you fail and get shipped off to die and this is the last time we spend together on nice dry land.' But when I thought about it, I really wanted to spend the evening with him too.

Raf walked me all the way to the bottom of the steps to my block and kissed me goodbye. We must have kissed for a while before we were finally interrupted by a friendly, 'OK, OK break it up then.' I looked up to see Marcus' smiling face and felt this shiver run through me. He acted like nothing had changed. Like he was still the friendly neighbourhood policeman. Like he'd done nothing wrong. And what was scariest was that I don't think it was an act. I think he genuinely thought he was one of the good guys.

There was no way we were going to keep snogging with Marcus watching us, so I gave Raf a quick hug goodbye and ran into the building. Dad was already upstairs; he'd finished work early specially.

'Come on,' he said, his face hard to read, a screwdriver in his hand. 'I've got something to show you.'

We went into his and Mum's room, me wondering if he'd finally cracked and was going to go all psycho with the screwdriver. I watched as he pushed the bed to one side and used the screwdriver to prise up a now exposed floorboard. And I'd thought we'd be making popcorn or chatting this evening.

Dad felt around in the hole under the floorboards and then smiled triumphantly and pulled up a dust-covered box with a super-large, super-grim spider on top. The spider fled. Dad stood up, sat on the bed and patted the duvet next to him.

I sat down.

'I wanted to tell you about Max,' Dad said quietly.

And for the next half hour Dad talked, pausing now and then to fish out another photo, blink back emotion or to give in to laughter, and I finally got to know the funny, kind, fiery uncle I'd never met. How he'd been really clever, saved Dad from loads of fights and always stood up to authority. He'd been against the idea of the Territory and the TAA and the idea of ranking kids. 'You remind me of him,' Dad continued. 'He was always so full of life and just so interested in everything. He liked to know how things worked and so he collected all sorts of stuff. Old gadgets, instruments and music, he was mad about music. When we were boys, we'd always sit in the same room. I'd be reading and he'd be listening to music and his foot always used to tap the floor in time and it'd drive me mad. He'd drive me so mad…' A sad sort of smile spread over Dad's face.

'This was his favourite gadget. Our granddad gave it to him. I think it was supposed to be a joke, but Max loved it.' Dad fished in the box again and pulled out this circle-shaped box. He held it out to me and I opened it. Inside sat a silver machine thing about the width of my palm with headphones attached. Dad opened it up to check 'if it had a disc in' and to 'put in some new batteries'.

'Put the headphones on and press the black button,' he said. The button had this arrow on. I raised one eyebrow but did what he said. There was a static noise and then the music started. Massively angry and loud and nothing like the music we got on our Scribes. The sort of music you have to dance to, but sort of fist-punch-in-the-air dancing. Not cool but you sort of have to. I got lost in it and got a massive shock when Dad tapped me on the shoulder and signalled to me to pull the headphones out.

'I'd like you to have it,' Dad said. 'I'd like you to have something of his.'

I was so touched.

'And here are some of his favourite discs.' I must have looked a bit dense as he explained, 'They've all got different music on. Different bands.'

'I can't wait to show everyone,' I said excitedly.

Dad looked unsure. 'Best keep it hidden, love. I'm pretty sure it's banned material. You don't want to be getting into trouble now.' He looked at his watch and seemed horrified it was so late. 'God, you'd better get back to studying, baby. Or your mum will kill me.'

I woke early from another nightmare. I'd been standing next to Jack in front of this massive clock. Marcus was facing us and had this psycho clown grin. He was pointing his gun from me to Jack and back again in time with this booming 'tick tock tick tock'. Marcus kept on grinning throughout and saying, 'Who shall I shoot, love?'

To shut out the images I reached under my mattress and pulled out Uncle Max's Discman. I listened to two whole discs before breakfast and by the time I met Daisy on the steps on the way into school, I had this weird faint ringing in my ears. We've started meeting on the steps most mornings so that we can at least catch up a bit before class. Her parents have banned us from even speaking on the phone at night, in case it, 'distracts her from her studies'.

I felt like I hadn't spoken to her for ages. Not properly. Jack too. It's like there's this gulf between us now. I can't tell them about Mum and the Laboratory as Raf and I had made a pact not to tell anyone. I didn't want to get Mum into trouble and truthfully I'm too big a coward to risk upsetting the Ministry. I don't want to disappear. Also the last thing Jack and Daisy need to worry about at the moment is becoming pustule-covered human experiments if they fail. Because they are likely victims after all. Neither of their parents would go with them. No one would know.

I searched for something to say. 'How's the neek?' I managed. Daisy just rolled her eyes and said, 'Gugh.' We both laughed but it was more for the sake of it than anything. There was no real joy in it.

I noticed that Daisy had a new necklace on. A gold butterfly on a pink ribbon. It looked small and discrete. In other words, massively expensive. Normally Daisy would have been strutting about showing it off, but this time she looked a bit small. Like a little girl wearing her mum's jewellery. When I asked her about it she said it was a present from her dad.

'But that's good, isn't it?' I said. 'If he's on side maybe he'll make your mum sack *Gugh* and we'll get to study together again for the final few days? It'll be like old times.'

Daisy shook her head. 'It's because he got a bonus,' she almost whispered.

I didn't get it at first. Just stared at her like a complete denser.

'A BIG bonus, Noa.'

I finally computed what she'd meant. A big bonus meant that the unaffordable was now affordable. The unimaginable now an option. My joint best friend in the whole world was going to get a late upgrade.

I stared a desperate, 'No way,' at her but Daisy just nodded.

'When?' was all I could manage.

'Tomorrow morning.'

It was like a blow to my stomach but much more painful than the actual blow Jack gave me that time. A sort of dull ache like a stone being lodged and twisted.

'That's soon.' I couldn't think of anything better to say.

'It's so they've got enough time to upload all the notes for the last five years. And then they do all these tests to check it's worked and the stuff's in my head.' Daisy instinctively rubbed the back of her neck as she spoke, then caught herself and did a little shiver. 'The surgeon's supposed to be really good. Dad says he's the best money can buy.' Daisy's voice was high and brittle with a trace of mania. 'God, Noa. They're actually going to make me one of them. They're going to turn me into a freakoid and there's nothing I can do to stop them.'

Daisy started sobbing uncontrollably, her body doing these frightening little spasm shakes.

I wanted to cry too. I wanted to rage and rant and scream. They were taking away my best friend. They were going to change her mind. Take the Daisy I knew and loved and leave a breathing shell with a computer brain. But I couldn't say any of this. I knew I just had to comfort her.

'Maybe it's OK.' I said, hugging her tight. 'At least you're going to pass now, right? Virtually guaranteed. No, stick that up your jumper. Actually guaranteed, as you're really bright to start with so now you'll be like super-you. And that's better than failing and being a Fish right? And they might put all this information into your head, but you'll still be Daisy. And I'll still be Noa. And we'll be best friends forever. And that will never change. OK?'

'Promise,' Daisy whispered. 'Promise they won't change me.'

'I promise,' I whispered back. What else could I say?

'Raf's a Childe and he's not like the other freakoids, is he?' Daisy's eyes craved reassurance. So I couldn't tell, could I? Couldn't tell her that Raf didn't upload. Couldn't tell her about his sister Chloe. Couldn't tell her anything.

'No, you'll be just like him, Daisy. Normal, just like him.' The lie almost stuck in my throat.

The only faintly OK thing was that Daisy was allowed out that evening. To come and study at mine. A bit like a last supper. I guess her mum thought that there was no need to keep her prisoner anymore, chained to her desk and a neek. Not now passing was in the bag. The worst that could happen is that her daughter would distract me, but Daisy's mum was way too selfish to let that concern her.

And Daisy and I did have an amazing evening. Well, as amazing as an evening could be that also contained three hours of Maths revision. Daisy was massively strict with me and made sure I studied with little breaks to chat to her. But those breaks were ACE. I felt closer to her than I have for ages. Since Raf turned up. We got out all these photo albums from way back and laughed at how tragic and young we used to look. Me, Daisy and Jack. Our three faces peering out again and again and again. Grinning, grinning, grinning. Three grinning monkeys.

'You know what?' Daisy said as we closed the final album and sat, curled up on my bed. 'I really thought you'd end up with Jack.'

'I guess I kind of did too,' I admitted. 'I'm not sure how or when or anything, but then Raf turned up and, well, you know.'

'Raf's cool too,' Daisy added.

'Yeah. He really is.'

'You so lurrrve him.' And I'd never been so pleased to hear one hundred per cent pure Daisy.

Maybe the late upgrade is actually a good thing. I mean, maybe it doesn't totally alter personality. Chloe could have been weird before, maybe Raf just didn't notice and Barnaby and Hugo are so massively different that it can't totally control behaviour. And Daisy was heading towards failing otherwise and then she could have ended up in the

Laboratory down some horrific corridor being experimented on. Lying there like Neil and Rosie. A lab rat with a number. As soon as I'd conjured up the image I had to try and block it but it just kept on eating into my thoughts.

I couldn't concentrate on anything today. Daisy's operation was at 11 am. That was in the middle of double Chemistry so I obviously took in none of that. I couldn't even talk to Raf at break. Raf's a big fan of Daisy and everything but he's not got the same connection, the same history, so the waiting just isn't the same for him. Jack looked about as worried as me and so we sort of agreed without talking, not to talk about it. Neither of us could face it. Maybe that's how telepathic powers develop.

I had lunch by myself. Surrounded by a sea of chattering voices, I had never felt more alone.

Hugo was out to provoke me. He'd made sure there was an empty stool next to him and he'd put a 'Reserved for Daisy' sign on it. I blinked back and breathed through the tears and managed to walk past him without the mask collapsing. Thankfully, Jack didn't see it or there'd have been a proper fight. And I'm talking broken jaws and everything.

Daisy said the operation would only take a couple of

hours and then there'd be recovery from the anaesthetic and then the tests. She reckoned she'd be done by early evening and home tomorrow.

Mum made me lasagne for dinner as special comfort food as she knew how difficult today was for me. It was comforting, although not quite the same as when we used to be able to put actual beef in it.

I tried to call the hospital after dinner and this was the weirdest. There was this really awkward pause and then they said Daisy had already been signed out. When I tried to ask how come she'd gone home so early, they just turned really cold and dismissive and said, 'We do not discuss our patients.'

But if Daisy was home she'd have called me, wouldn't she? I mean it's slightly different, but when she had her appendix out three years ago, she called me literally as soon as she got through the door.

I tried calling Jack to see if he'd heard anything. He hadn't. He'd tried the hospital too and got the same response.

'Maybe she's home but still a bit out of it from the operation,' he suggested, but I could tell from his voice that he realised how lame this sounded.

'If it was something like that, she'd still be in hospital. They don't just send you home early when you're still drugged up,' I insisted. 'Not when you've spent *that* amount of money. And, anyway, they can't send you home till they've done all the tests to check it's worked and they couldn't do that if she was at all out of it.'

'OK, Noa, OK.' I guess I'd made my point a bit too clearly.

There was a long pause. I needed to search for strength to share my next thoughts. 'It's happened, hasn't it, Jack? They've got to her. They've turned her into a proper freakoid like Logan and now she doesn't want anything to do with us.'

Jack's silent agreement was more than I could take and I hung up and threw the phone to the floor. It bounced up and down on its coiled cord before hanging, lifeless, from its socket in the corridor.

Mum started to get worried about the level of crying coming from my room. She knows there isn't exactly time to have a night off revision.

'Call her, Noa-bean. If you're this worried, stop over-analysing it and just call her home. I'm sure everything will be OK. And at least you'll know.' But maybe I didn't want to. Not if it was as bad as I thought.

I knew Mum was right though and I picked up the phone again, a slight tremor in my right hand. It rang eleven times. Then there was Daisy's mum's clipped voice as the answerphone message kicked in.

'The best that money can buy' is a malc phrase that means nothing.

The surgeon's hand slipped.

He'd been drinking the night before and still had alcohol in his system. Ten times the Medical Council limit. Which doesn't actually make sense if you think about it, as surely the limit if you're putting a massively sharp scalpel next to someone's massively important spinal cord should be a big fat zero and ten times zero is still zero.

It's an 'open and shut case of medical negligence' according to Dad. Daisy's family will get compensation: the cost of the upgrade refunded plus twenty thousand Golds in damages. And that's what most people seem concerned with. How much money her family will get. As if it's something good. A lottery win. Not the fact that Daisy's been turned into a vegetable. Not that she was completely and totally brain-damaged. Not that Daisy's parents decided there and then to switch off life support so I didn't even get to say goodbye.

And the worst thing is that I bet Daisy's mum is probably actually quite pleased. Not that she'd admit it. But in private, if she was sure no one was looking, she'd probably allow herself as much of a smile as her overly botoxed face would allow. More money, less responsibility. One pure freakoid child with impeccable credentials. No slightly embarrassing lesser model late upgrade. Logan too wouldn't care less as he's incapable of any human emotion. Daisy's dad would be upset for a millisecond, but then he'd just go back to working twenty hours a day and forget she even existed. No one would really miss her. No one but me and Jack. And this thought pushed my despair to anger. And anger's better. I can hold onto in. Burn with it.

I went to Raf's after school. I needed to be held, to be kissed, to forget, if just for a second. Raf probably thinks I'm seriously weird and psycho now, as in the middle of kissing him, I slapped his face, then grabbed him close, then bit his lip and then grabbed him again and then broke down into tears, rocking on the floor and moaning quietly.

He picked me up and held me tight, rocking me and singing to me while stroking my hair. Mid sobs I tried to tell him that I loved him.

He just put his finger over my lips and kept singing.

When I got home, Mum said Jack had called about ten times. I know I should be there for him. Shouldn't leave him all alone with his grief. He hasn't got a Raf equivalent to cry on. But I can't reopen the wound. My body just can't handle more crying. I'm numb. Empty. I crawled into bed, my Geography notes on the Arable Lands untouched on my desk. For the first time I'm behind on my revision schedule.

And the thing is I really don't care.

I hadn't been to church since a school trip in Year Three.

Mum and Dad are massive atheists and for some weird reason, spires used to creep me out. I think they reminded me of pointy witches' fingers clawing at the sky. I used to have a real phobia about witches. Witches and big fish.

Anyway, I couldn't study however much I stared at the page. Words were just like pointless symbols my brain couldn't deal with. I needed to say goodbye to Daisy, to go somewhere to mourn her. There wasn't even going to be a proper funeral and I was starting to feel claustrophobic in my room.

I waited until the 11am main service had finished and then crept in through the church's side entrance, feeling like an intruder. The chill coming off the stone pillars was somehow comforting and the massively high ceiling seemed to give space to think. There was a row of candles down one end, with a lighter, a knife to trim the wax and a donations box. I put half a Gold in the box and reached for the lighter. The flame looked so gentle above the white candle. Graceful and beautiful. Like Daisy? No, Daisy was more than that. She was cool and fun and sparky and loyal. She kicked beautiful and graceful's ass.

I didn't know how to pray. How to even start to go about it. So I just sat the candle in the rack and gazed at it while thinking back through my favourite memories of Daisy. I thought of the moment we first claimed best friends status when we were ten. We'd spent the day at the Park learning to hula hoop and blow bubble gum. Daisy was obviously way better than me at hula-ing but my bubbles aced hers. That is until I blew one so big that it burst and went all over my face and fringe. It wouldn't come out of my fringe and so Daisy decided we'd have to cut out the gum. She produced this pair of scissors from her bag and hacked a big chunk out of my fringe. I started going mental, knowing that I now looked like a complete denser, but Daisy just laughed and hacked a matching chunk out of her own fringe, saying, 'We'll look ridiculous together, best friends forever.'

I don't know why I thought this would be a good idea, but something made me reach out for the knife by the candles. Trembling slightly, I used it to cut off a lock of my hair, sawing as the blade was so blunt. I held my hair in the flame and watched it burn from golden to charred black, tears streaming down my face.

I know I should have gone to Jack's then. Or at least include him in my improvised memorial service. I even started walking to his house when I left the church. But then my feet almost automatically took a right instead of a left and I ended up back at Raf's. In his arms.

I did the most terrible thing today. I betrayed Raf and I can't do anything to take it back.

I hadn't talked to Jack since Daisy's death and I knew things were going to be difficult. As soon as I saw him enter the classroom, I could tell he was in the foulest mood ever. From the frown criss-crossing his forehead, to his searchlight eyes, to the way he was hunching his shoulders, it was as if a dark vortex of anger was spiralling above his head, ready to engulf us all. OK, that sounds massively dramatic and it wasn't quite like that, but looking back, it should have been.

He caught my eye and then looked away. Determined to talk to him and massively guilt-driven at having abandoned him over the weekend, I went up to his desk. He was sat facing away from me, staring at a knot of wood in front of him. I ruffled his hair. He normally likes this. It's one of our things. He didn't like it today, just pushed me away.

'Where were you?' Jack spat, turning to face me. 'I needed you. I needed to talk. About Daisy. I called. I kept on calling.' Anger started to turn to overwhelming sadness. Which was even worse. 'Where were you, Noa?' He sounded like Rex when he'd had this huge splinter in his paw. His eyes were the same too.

'I'm sorry, Jack. I should have called. I know I should have called. I'm so, so sorry. But I'm here now.'

'Were you with him?' Jack's voice was scarily neutral.

Silence.

'Well were you?' His eyes were now more Ms Jones on a caffeine pill than Rex.

I nodded.

Jack half snorted, half bark-laughed. 'That's SO typical, you know, Noa. You act like you're this GREAT friend. Like you're SO concerned. Like you'll help your STUPID friends revise when it suits you as it makes you feel better and cleverer. But at the end of the day, you really don't give a crap. It's all about you, always has been. You're like a freakoid. No, I take it back. You're worse than a freakoid. At least they don't pretend to care and then throw it all back in your face.'

I couldn't quite believe I was hearing this. I'd never heard Jack speak like this. Never. Tears started forming behind my eyes but I manically blinked them back.

'I guess I should have seen it coming. I mean when it comes down to it, no Norm is good enough for you. Not me, who you treat like some kind of toy. And certainly not Daisy. I mean Noa, seriously, Daisy's been there for you your whole life, but you don't even have time to mourn her as you're too busy snogging your new freakoid boyfriend.'

Maybe anger's catching. Either way, I could feel it flow

through me, cell by cell. I was aware we had quite an audience by now, but it was like the play button was jammed and I couldn't stop.

'How can you seriously stand there and say this crap?' I shouted back. 'Do you really think I don't care what's happened to Daisy? What they've done to my best friend? I mean, really? And you – I've always been there for you, always.'

'Not since you've met Mr Robot, you've haven't. What's he's got, exactly? Do you secretly want to be a freakoid. Is that it? Do you get a kinky sort of thrill as you watch him plug in? Turns you on, does it, Noa?'

'Shut up! Just shut up right now! You don't know what you're talking about. Raf's an amazing guy. A better and smarter person than you'll ever be.'

'Yeah, 'cos life's really hard when you upload isn't it? He's got enough time to entertain you, does he? Does better than me in tests, does he? What a surprise!'

'He doesn't even upload!' The words were out of my mouth before they even registered in my brain. Floating across the air of the classroom. Like poison gas.

A deathly silence fell. Everyone turned to look at me and then at Raf, whose presence I suddenly became aware of. He must have just come in. I willed Raf to look at me, but he just stared past, expressionless, chewing gum.

I don't know when Ms Jones entered the room, but she made herself known with a sudden intake of breath. Like she was hoovering up all the discomfort and fear in the room and feeding off it. Her eyes sparkled dangerously. She'd never liked Raf. She'd marked him out as different. And now she knows why.

'Noa Blake, is this true?'

I stood immobile, not knowing what to do.

'Noa, answer me truthfully. If you lie, I WILL know and I'll deduct another five points from your TAA score.' Everyone sucked in their breath at that. Five points was unheard of. Five points was a death sentence.

Before I could answer Raf stood up. 'It's true,' he said. 'I didn't upload for the last test.'

'And may I ask why?' Ms Jones' words were honey-coated venom. 'Are you above your fellow Childes? It is almost as if you don't trust the information we are providing you with? Is it that, Rafael? Do you not trust the uploads?'

Raf was very still and pale but I could see the battle raging inside him. To admit he didn't trust the uploads would be seen as an attack on the system and mark him out as a Subversive. To say he did trust the uploads would be a direct lie.

Raf did what was necessary. What I would have done. He lied. 'My Port's broken at the moment,' he muttered. 'It's being mended. It won't happen again.'

'Well, that's good to hear.' Ms Jones smiled. She's most dangerous when she's smiling. 'Then you won't mind coming with me to the library for a catch-up upload. To check that you have this year's material correctly stored.'

And then she led him out of the room. And that's when he finally looked at me, his eyes like Mr Patel's when he had seen the baton rise, when he knew it was too late to run.

I couldn't help myself. I followed Ms Jones and Raf to the library. He was half-hidden by a screen but I could still see. See her sit him by a Port. See her bend down to pick up the wire and hand it to Raf. See him with his hand in front of his mouth, almost gagging, before taking it and plugging it in. Then his eyes went all white and he sat and shook for a solid ten minutes until Ms Jones declared, 'That's enough,' and unplugged him. He sat limp. As if the lifeforce had been sucked out of him. Then he took one big breath. Then another. Then another. And with each breath his back became straighter; his head held higher.

He stood up and started the walk back to the classroom. This time he walked shoulder to shoulder with Ms Jones: her equal rather than her victim.

I followed, a lame shadow, trying to telepath out a connection. As Raf turned to enter the classroom, he looked at me. Directly in the eye.

'Raf,' was all I could manage.

His expression was stone. No spark in his eye. No trace of wolf in his face.

'Out of my way, Norm.'

Five days to go now. God! This must be what it feels like to be on Death Row. At least there you get to choose a final meal. Mine would definitely not include mucor or any form of algae. And death is quick. Well, used to be. According to Jack's step-dad, they're apparently stopping trying criminals and will just dump them in the Wetlands instead. Prisons and courts are a waste of dry land. As if Fish don't have enough to deal with. What's worse, Jack's step-dad mentioned it like it was some great news 'cos it's his transport company that'll probably get the contract to do the dumping.

I don't know if it's possible to cram any more. It seems that I'm now so saturated with facts that everytime I try and put something new in my brain, something I've already learnt pops out. Mum keeps on telling me to take a break. But seriously? NO ONE takes a break with two days to go, even if they've just lost their boyfriend and their best friend has died. I guess the will to survive is pretty strong.

Another unwelcome fact from Jack (presumably via his step-dad again): six per cent of students suffer seizures from lack of sleep on one or both of the exam days and four per cent try to kill themselves by shoving styluses up their noses and then ramming their heads down on their desk. Goes straight through the brain. Apparently. I think

Jack felt guilty at sharing this choice information when he saw how ready to puke I looked.

'I thought it'd cheer you up,' he said.

'Denser.'

'What I was trying to say is that's ten per cent of the competition gone.'

And I nearly smiled and was actually a bit pleased when I registered this. What sort of sick people have we become?

Jack studied here tonight. He's my rock again. Which I guess means I've been reduced to a limpet.

I hated him. Violently hated him after what happened to Raf. But then I realised that it was really just me that I hated. After all, it was me not Jack who'd betrayed Raf. Me that'd effectively killed him and given them an empty body to freakoid up. And Jack was so devastated by what happened. So we just sort of comforted each other. And it feels like the return of a lost limb. It's nice. An oasis of nice in the middle of a big load of nasty.

Time studying is also time not thinking about Raf or Daisy. Which is good. Necessary. Or I might start shoving styluses up my nose. Seeing Raf is so hard. And that means every day is so hard as he's in nearly all my classes. I swear I caught him staring at me in Geography yesterday. Jack was rubbing my back as I had a massive stress knot and Raf's eyes went all narrow and slity like a wolf that wasn't sexy but that might actually eat you. I nearly cried there and then like a right loser at the level of hate or contempt he felt for me. Knowing that I was now just a Norm to him. A nobody. And he, even in spite of the upload, was still such a somebody to me.

Tonight I just want to sleep. No dreams, just oblivion.

I read *The Diary of Anne Frank* when I was ten. It's not on our Scribes, but Dad had a really old copy from when he was young. He said I should read it as it was 'a lesson in amazing bravery'.

'Anne's bravery?' I remember asking.

'Yes, that too, but also that of the family that protected her and hid her from the Nazis.'

And I remember thinking, but surely that's just what anyone who's not an evil Jew-murdering Nazi would do, isn't it?

We were woken at 1am by the knock at the door. Rap. Once. Pause. Then rap, rap. Twice. Then rap, once, again. Then rap, rap, rap, rap, rap, each knock like a short staccato note. Long pause. Then the whole sequence was repeated again. As my still half-asleep brain began to process what going on, I could feel adrenaline begin to pump around my body in time with the knocks. It was the code. Ella and Aunty Vicki's emergency code. By the time I had my dressing gown on and was staggering out into the main room, I could hear Mum and Dad arguing.

'Don't open the door, Rachel,' Dad was urging. 'You already know what they want and we can't. We just can't.'

'They're family. We can't just bolt out family.'

'Rachel, no! Think of Noa. She's got one more day at home till her exams. She doesn't need this. You're putting her at risk too.'

It was too late, Mum had already pulled back the bolt and opened the door.

Ella and Aunty Vicki's faces peered in, almost ghostly white against the black corridor. Something about their faces made me think of twin rabbits. Albino rabbits in the biology lab cage at school.

Mum ushered them in and then checked and rechecked the corridor for witnesses.

'No one saw us, Rachel,' Aunty Vicki said. 'The policeman was patrolling the other end of the street.'

'What about the camera on the ground floor?' Mum asked Aunty Vicki, her voice little more than a whisper.

Aunty Vicki held up a hammer and balaclava by way of explanation.

'It's broken.'

There was this really long static silence.

'I'll make tea,' Dad said and sidled off into the kitchen,

shooting Mum looks so they could have one of their telepathic conversations.

'Noa, take Ella into your room. Aunty Vicki and I need to talk. Alone.'

Ella followed me, head lowered. She sat, hands clutching ankles, a foetal ball at the bottom of my bed. And slowly the story spilled out.

Ella was going to fail. She was sure of it. Aunty Vicki had decided to risk the week's rations and keep her out of school on Friday to sit four past papers. She'd got 32 per cent in Maths, 51 per cent in Biology, 37 per cent in Physics and 43 per cent in Geography. There was no way she'd make 70 per cent on the following Saturday. Even if she aced the other subjects. Just no way. Aunty Vicki had made the decision as they'd gone through the mark schemes together, Ella's face a mess of mascara-coated tears. She wasn't going to give away her daughter without a fight. Stand by and watch her pack her last suitcase. Let them take her to the Waiting Place. Pile her into one of the 'resettlement' buses to be taken off to die. She'd go with her if it came to it. But they'd run first.

It had taken them three days to get here. Travelling by night. Crawling along ditches, sleeping in skips. Ella's left heel was a mass of weeping blisters. No one should have noticed their disappearance yet. No one tended to run before the exams. I mean, if there was the minutest chance you'd pass, you wouldn't, would you? Running itself is an

'Act of Opposition' and fugitives ALWAYS got caught, well Norms anyway.

'Mum was thinking we could hide here,' Ella continued. 'They probably wouldn't check, would they? I mean with your mum working for the Ministry and everything. And then we could go and live in the Arable Lands or hide out in the Solar Fields or something. That Archie guy managed to get by for a year before he was caught and he was basically the stupidest guy ever.'

I just sat there like a denser. A mute denser. I wanted to say, 'Yes stay.' I wanted to say, 'You can hide in my wardrobe. We'll feed you. We'll protect you. You're family.' But my throat wouldn't release the words. And all I was really thinking was my wardrobe's tiny and if you stay they'll come looking and they'll find you and then we'll all die and I really, really don't want to die.

Suddenly we heard shouting from the main room and the sound of things smashing over and over. Ella and I ran to open my door and saw Dad grabbing Aunty Vicki by the wrists as she brandished the hammer at Mum, who was surrounded by a sea of broken mugs and furniture.

All three turned to look at us.

Aunty Vicki spoke first.

'OK we're going. We're going. Ella, get your things. The plan's changed.'

Ella's face was fear itself. Her whole body seemed to crumple. 'But…' she began to stutter.

'There's no time,' Aunty Vicki continued. 'We'll be OK, sweetheart. I'll protect you, baby,' and then her voice broke and she roughly pushed tears away.

Tears streamed down Mum's face too as she shut the door behind them.

'They're not staying then?' I said, just to say something.

'No … they're not.' And then she said, 'Oh God, I love you, Noa-bean,' just like she used to when she tucked me up in bed when I was really small.

Then I started crying too. Crying because of what was going to happen to Ella and Aunty Vicki. Crying because I was so relieved that we weren't going to risk hiding them. And crying because I felt so guilty at how selfish I am.

I would have killed Anne Frank.

So many lasts in just one day.

Last weekend.

Last day of walking down the streets, hand in hand with Jack.

Potentially last dinner at home. EVER EVER EVER.

Dinner was awful. Truly awful. Mum and Dad were trying so hard to be fun and to ignore what was going to happen tomorrow and what had happened last night that they were like weird wind-up clowns or people in some freaky horror or body-swap film. Mum must have used up about five days' rations to prepare a feast, but it kept on just getting stuck in my throat and I had to choke every mouthful down. It might as well have been mucor. I don't know what they're going to eat for the rest of the week. And they kept talking about plans for the rest of the year and for next year and the year after. As if by repeatedly denying even the possibility that I'd get sent away that'd somehow stop it happening. Like a magic mantra or something.

I broke halfway through pudding. Dad was talking about going on this big family trip to the Woods for my sixteenth birthday and I just stood up and screamed, 'Shut up, shut up, shut up!' and ran to my room.

A few minutes later, Mum tapped at my door and sheepishly shuffled in.

'Sorry, Mum,' I whispered, peeping out from under my duvet.

'No, we're sorry, baby. We just wanted you to have a nice evening. To feel that everything was normal and will be normal.'

'But it's not normal, is it, Mum? It couldn't exactly be further from normal. Daisy's dead, Raf's a freakoid, Ella and Aunty Vicki are no doubt already being hunted down by the police and I'm probably going to fail the TAA and get sent off to die and never see you and Dad again.' Huge sobs just seemed to burst out of my body without my brain even sending signals.

'Stop right there,' Mum said, her voice comfort with a steel core. 'You are my brilliant daughter. You will sail through these exams.'

'But I might not, Mum. Please, just for once, acknowledge that I might not.'

She took a deep breath and exhaled. I knew how much these words would cost her.

'OK. Suppose these examiners are morons.' Mum never says morons. 'Suppose you do fail. Dad and I are coming with you. We'll be sitting next to you on the bus and sleeping next to you in the shelter we'll build with you there.'

I almost smiled at the idea of Mum and Dad building a shelter. They're both beyond useless at DIY.

'But you shouldn't die too.'

'We won't die. The Blakes are survivors. And if you're not here, Noa, there's nothing left for us in the Territory anyway.'

Then she helped me pack.

On my bed's my bag. Still quite slim, innocuous looking. On the top's the massively anal sheet specifying exactly what I'm supposed to take, the Ministry's crappy symbol at the top.

'Revision aids;

7 pairs of undergarments;

2 pairs of trousers;

4 tops/shirts;

2 jumpers;

1 pair of shoes (waterproof)

Sufficient to provide for the two Exam Days and the Waiting Place.'

The bus pulled up at the stop three minutes early. Everyone was already there, waiting; a crocodile of students, parents and suitcases lining the grey pavement. It had just started to rain. Eyelashes blinked away raindrops and tears as we boarded, one by one, Ms Jones grimly ticking off names on her tightly clasped clipboard. Even the freakoids looked slightly freaked out as if some human feelings were finally surfacing.

You could tell a lot about families by how they said goodbye and good luck. Hugo's mum gave Hugo a cold peck on the cheek and his dad gave him a clipped handshake. I guess they knew there was no way that Hugo wasn't coming back, so why waste emotion? Raf's mum gave him a huge hug; his dad hadn't even bothered to show. I knew how much that would bother him. Or maybe I didn't. Maybe new robotic Raf wouldn't even care anymore. In any event, he avoided me, as usual, even after I swear I saw his mum point me out. Jack's mum rubbed Jack's head into her chest, which might have looked really affectionate, if massively inappropriate, but was really just to draw more attention to her saggy cleavage and to make sure her carefully applied and over-bright lipstick didn't smudge.

Mum and Dad were the best. They were sandwiched either side of me, stroking my hair, singing stupid songs, including the classic, 'Noa, Noa, Noa Blake' to the tune of *Twinkle Twinkle Little Star*. Normally I would have found this the most cringeworthy thing ever. But this morning I kind of liked it and willed them not to stop.

Finally it was my turn to board. The driver took my suitcase and threw it into the hold. I dragged myself up the five steps, my legs like lead weights. Jack had saved me a seat towards the back and I burrowed in next to him.

'Thanks,' I whispered. It was the sort of morning that everyone was speaking at half volume.

'No probs. Couldn't have you sitting at the front like a loser.'

I punched Jack in the arm and he grinned. His grin was ACE. Then he dove into his rucksack and produced his Scribe and his headphones to share.

I looked around to check Ms Jones was still busy at the front and then produced my discman. He laughed at me as if I'd pulled out some sort of museum exhibit.

'Shut up,' I hissed. 'I know it looks ridiculous but the music's good. Different. I wanted you to listen to it.'

'You're making this up, Noa.'

'Just listen, but make sure no one sees.'

Jack laughed again and said that no one would care what we were listening to now. Everyone knew this was probably a one-way trip. My mood dropped even lower, if possible.

'God, sorry, I'll shut up now.' Jack said apologetically. 'And I meant for me. Not you. You're definitely going back. You're like a natural super-brain.' My stare must have got more intense and glum as Jack put his hands up and said, 'OK, OK, change of topic. Right, let's listen to your music then.' I fast-forwarded to my favourite track and the song started. The one where the singer just keeps on repeating, 'You sent me away, now I'm gonna make you pay!!' and it really seemed to capture and intensify all my mixed-up feelings of fear and anger – yes, above all I guess, huge boiling anger against the Ministry for taking us away and putting us through this. Jack and I were soon singing along and row upon row turned round to stare at us in total confusion. We looked at each other and just totally cracked up. Lost it. Tears running down our faces although we both knew it wasn't really THAT funny, it was just a release.

Ms Jones' voice cut through the laughter. 'Noa and Jack, stop this noise immediately.'

Jack and I just burst out laughing again. I mean what could she do to us now? There was an unwritten policy against deducting points at this late stage. Seen as too cruel, I guess.

The rest of the journey to the Waiting Place was pretty uneventful. We finally turned into the driveway at just after 4pm. I don't know if it was just our mood, but as the tyres first crunched gravel, the clouds seemed to grow darker and darker and everyone seemed to shrink a little into their seats. The Waiting Place was massive. Like a factory, or a prison. Large, grey and squat, with loads of barbed wire and high railings. And this was supposed to be one of the nice ones. Waiting Place 12 to be precise – reserved for students from the most prestigious private schools. I guess pre-Archie Rycroft, freakoids got to stay at home and just bus in for the actual exams, so maybe standards were pretty low. I mean a fee-paying Norm's still just a Norm. I'd hate to see what the other ones were like though.

Hugo's voice could be heard complaining, 'My dad will have something to say to the Governing Body about this dump,' but everyone else was mute, awed by the slab of a building that was going to be 'home' for the next five days. Even Ms Jones seemed slightly cowed and spoke reasonably gently with a tinge of – could it be? – pity in her voice as she told us to get out.

We trudged through two sets of thick steel gates that made a threatening 'clung' as bolts slid in and out of place and then we were inside. Rooms were allocated randomly and Jack and I were each in a single-sex dorm of eight.

A Waiting Place Attendant — think *guard* — filled us

in on the programme — think *drill*. Dinner was at 6pm; lights out at 9.30pm; wake-up call for tomorrow's exam 6.30am, breakfast 7am, exam start 8.30am. The rest of this evening was 'Free Time' to be spent in our allocated room or Communal Study Area 5C.

We formed another sorry crocodile and were marched to our rooms. Luckily, Jack's and mine were on the same corridor. Jack's positivity and rebellious energy seemed to have evaporated inside the building. Like it had been sucked out of him by 360 degrees of concrete. I recognised the knotted lines in his forehead and knew that exam panic was building.

I dumped my suitcase on the end of my hard bed and looked around at my fellow roommates: three Norms and four freakoids. If I didn't know, I don't think I could actually have definitely told the difference. Everyone seemed shy and a bit withdrawn. Maybe the Ministry hadn't developed an upload that could totally eradicate exam fear.

I got out my Scribe and my flash cards (which sent a few eyebrows rising) and, sitting cross-legged on the bed, started to revise in earnest. I figured if I ate dinner really fast, I had time for 30 mins History, 30 mins Biology, 30 mins Maths, 30 mins Geography and 30 mins Physics. Jack and I had agreed to study separately. I tried to talk him into letting me help, at least with the Physics, but he'd insisted. Said it was 'everyone for themselves', but I know it was really because he knew I'd get through more without him and he wanted me to pass. I think he might even want me to pass more than himself.

We didn't talk in the dinner hall. I forced mucor and some form of sweetened algae down, realising I needed all the fuel I could get to get through the next few days. I thought of Mum. She always used to feed me fish fingers before exams. Brain food, she used to say. That is, until all the fish got diseased. I quickly pushed such thoughts aside. They weren't helpful. Not now.

As I was queuing to leave the hall I heard a painfully familiar voice behind me. 'Noa.' I thought I must be hearing things. I turned and there, sure enough, was Raf. My heart leapt. I thought that maybe I'd got it all wrong. Maybe they hadn't totally freakoided him. Maybe he still cared. He seemed about to speak again when he was suddenly flanked by Hugo and Quentin.

'What do you want with the Norm?' Hugo sneered. 'I thought you were over Fish Face here.'

Raf's face became stone. 'Of course I am,' was his cold reply. 'I just thought she could help me relieve some stress before the exams, you know. Everyone knows Norms are easy.'

Hugo and Quentin sniggered like, well, like sniggering freakoids and I forced myself not to cry. How could I have thought he might still like me? I'm an idiot, idiot, idiot.

When everyone else piled towards the Communal Study

Area (where there were zillions of Ports in case you'd missed any uploads), I headed back to the dorm, to study alone on my bed. I channelled all my anger at Raf into super-concentration mode and read flash card after flash card until the lights went out. After all, every minute counts.

How can you describe a day like today?

The exams? Honestly, I have no idea. It's too close to call.

The exam hall was massive. Rows and rows of students — must have been at least ten different schools' worth. And we were arranged alphabetically rather than by school so you had to sit in this sea of strange faces. Face after face you didn't know. It really brought home how many people we're competing against. Before, it was always that I had to beat or at least be as good as Hugo and Quentin and Barnaby, but today there were hundreds of Hugos and Quentins and Barnabys and they all looked pretty clever in a freakoidy way. And if that wasn't stressful enough, positioned all round the room and down the dividing aisles were guards. Guards in uniform. With guns. And then before the first exam, Maths, even started, this super-scary invigilator guy stood up and declared that there had been, 'an erratum' on page twelve. 'Triangles' should read 'triangle'. I mean?! We could have worked that out. It's much easier to figure that out than to try and figure out what the hell 'erratum' means. Why couldn't they just say error or, let's go crazy, *mistake*, like any normal person? I swear they get some sort of perverted kick out of it.

I think Maths was OK. There was one horrific question at the end that I had to leave out, but that was bound to happen and that was only 5 per cent of the total. There were some others I was a bit unsure of, but although I won't have got the 90 per cent that I really wanted to boost my marks in other subjects, I should have cleared 70 per cent.

Geography wasn't so good. It was basically all recall so the freakoids are going to ace it. IT'S SO UNFAIR! There was also a long question on the Arable Lands that I hadn't revised well as it'd come up last year so I'd assumed it wouldn't this year. Supremely annoying! Physics and Biology were OK, especially as there were lots of questions on circuits and classification, which I'm quite strong on.

History is the one I'm freaking out about a bit. We had to write an essay on the Dark Times and how life is better now, which is really hard to do. I'm not a denser, so obviously I wrote about everything being great now and terrible then but I didn't have any statistics to back it up and I'm worried that maybe I tried too hard and over-compensated and it sounded really insincere.

After the exams had finished, all I could think of was finding Jack. Seeing how he'd found it. Physics and Biology are two of his worst subjects, but then there hadn't been much on magnetism or genetics (his two massively weak areas) so maybe he'd be OK. I just wanted him to tell me that he'd be fine. That we'd both be fine and get to stay. I couldn't find him in the dinner hall or his dorm and then like some brain worm, horrific images of him shoving a stylus up his nose and banging his head down kept burrowing into my head. The only other place I could think of to check was the men's toilets. Maybe he was trying to drown himself in the bowl or strangle himself using the flush chain. Shut up, brain! I checked no one was in the corridor and then sidled into the men's. No one was at the urinals but there was a cubicle, locked and I could hear rustling inside.

'Jack!' I shouted, beginning to pound on the door in my panic. 'Don't do it, Jack.'

There was no response.

'Jack, open that door or I'll kick it in right now!'

'That's something I'd like to see,' came a voice from behind the door. It wasn't Jack's.

I mumbled some sort of noise of incomprehension and the lock slid back.

'Well, get in here. Quick about it. And don't scream.'

Part of me wanted to run, but something stopped me. I pushed the door. One blue eye, one green. Raf dragged me inside and locked the door.

I tried not to panic, my ears straining for other sounds outside the door. There was nothing. We were very much alone.

Taking a deep breath, I forced myself to look him straight in the eye. No flinching. Maybe I could unlock some buried memory of us together. Maybe I could stop him hurting me. At least I was in position to try some sort of eye gauging manoeuvre.

I was expecting to see danger in his face. But there were no glinting eyes. Not even a hungry wolf's grin. Instead I saw pain. He might even have been blinking away a tear.

'Noa.' It was almost like he'd breathed the word. 'God, I've missed you.'

Raf. He was back.

'What the hell is going on?' I asked, trying to sound angry, but there was the old Raf grin and eye sparkle. 'I mean I saw you upload. I saw what they did to you. I watched you become a monster.'

'It was just an act.'

'But I saw you plug in and twitch for God's sake. I saw it all.'

'You saw what I wanted you to see. What I needed everyone to see. I've got a freakoid sister. I've watched enough people upload to know how to fake it. I'm sorry, Noa, it was the only way to keep us both safe.'

The tears welled up in my eyes, and I found myself punching him repeatedly as hard as I could. Laughing and crying and angry all at the same time. Then something struck me.

'But the upload…' I stammered.

He pulled a piece of gum out of his mouth. 'I pushed it into my Node when I inserted the cable.'

'Gum? But how did you know it'd work … that it wouldn't short the circuit or blow the Port or something?'

'I didn't,' Raf replied grimly. And it all started to make sense – what he'd done. The risk he'd taken – for both of us.

'I'm sorry, Noa. I hated myself for having to act like that, say those things. And all I wanted to do all the time was wrap my arms round you, kiss you, ask you how you were holding up. I wanted it to be me looking after you, not Jack, but imagine what they'd do if they found out I'd deceived them and that you knew. They can't be made to look like fools, Noa. We'd both have been sent to the Wetlands immediately. We wouldn't even get to sit this exam.'

I knew he was right.

And then he wrapped his arms round me, drew me close and started to kiss me. And I kissed him back, harder than ever. It felt like everything was back to normal. Well, almost.

'When did you start hiding out in toilets?'

'Well, I'd heard that Norms were easy so I thought I'd hang about and see if I could get some Norm toilet cubicle action.' I punched him again.

'If you keep that up you're going to get a sore hand.'

I landed another punch, putting my full weight into it.

'Ow, OK, OK, I'm sorry, I couldn't resist. I'm here because I'm revising,' Raf laughed.

'In a toilet cubicle?'

'Well, I can't exactly be seen studying in my room can I as I'm supposed to be a proper freakoid now, as you'd put it, and us freakoids don't stare at notes all evening. And I don't know about you, but I've got a pretty serious set of exams tomorrow.'

Mention of exams suddenly brought us back to reality with a bang.

I needed to be studying and I needed to find Jack.

I kissed him again.

'I missed you so much,' I murmured into his neck.

'Me too. Me too,' he replied.

'By the way, how did they go?'

'OK, I think. Yes, kind of OK.'

'Me too. I think'

We left separately, and hadn't heard anyone else come into the men's so our secret should be safe. I eventually found Jack in the communal revision room, staring intently at notes for tomorrow's exams.

'How did it go?' I asked. 'I was so worried about you! I thought you might even have done something stupid,' and I told him about my toilet suicide theory (minus the Raf bit), which made him laugh.

'No. I've got to stay around to look after you, right?' The intensity of feeling in his voice made me feel massively guilty. 'I don't know how I did, not great. But maybe good enough. Who knows.' Hope shone through his smile and my heart leapt. 'You obviously aced it though.'

'What?'

'Well, just look at you. You're beaming.'

They're over. Just like that. All that work, that cramming for just two days.

And now it's probably all over for me too. Because I'm stupid, stupid, stupid.

Maybe I suffered burn-out, maybe my brain was on Raf rather than Chemistry or maybe I'm just a natural denser after all, but for whatever dumb reason I double turned over. The most obvious, stupidest mistake anyone could make in an exam. I missed out two whole sides of questions. High-mark questions on bonding and calculations. That's at least 30 per cent of the marks. It'd be better not to know. I was checking through the paper at the end, feeling SMUG, can you believe it?! Smug that I'd finished with so much time to spare. I'd even indulged in a little daydream about going on a trip to the Woods with Raf when this was all over. Strolling in dappled glades. Throwing leaves at each other. Idiot. Just as the invigilator said, 'Pens down,' I opened the empty pages and nearly puked from fear.

'NO!' I must have shouted aloud as all eyes turned to face me and the invigilator hiss-shouted, 'Silence. All eyes to the front.'

My paper was collected with all the others and my stomach started to eat itself.

The afternoon's exams were a bit of a blur. English was OK. I think my essay hung together and made sense and I included loads of 'powerful' verbs and 'persuasive' language. Art was a bit of a joke as I'm rubbish even at scale drawing, but all I could/can think about was the Chemistry paper and those blank pages.

When the bell to mark the end of the final exam tolled, I couldn't join in the yells and mad celebrations that seemed to break out. I caught sight of Jack's face in the distance. Tired but kind of relieved and almost happy looking, so he must have had an OK day, which I'm so pleased about. I couldn't face him though. Didn't want to talk about it as talking would just make it even more real. I slipped down a side corridor and shunning dinner, headed back to my dorm knowing I'd get a few minutes peace there, at least until everyone had finished eating.

Solitude didn't seem to help either though. I pounded my pillow and then started sobbing into it. It wasn't only me that I'd doomed. It was my entire family. Mum and Dad are as stubborn as I am and would insist on coming with me. Results Day was in just two days and after that I'd never see Raf again either. Just thinking his name was enough to get me bawling again. I needed him.

For no massively logical reason, I started sprinting down the corridor to the men's. Hoping he'd somehow be in there again. The cubicle was occupied and I ran up to it, and knocked.

'What the hell?' came a reedy, nasally voice. Not Raf's. Of course it wasn't Raf's. What was I thinking?

Feeling even more of an idiot, I slunk back down the corridor to my dorm. I kicked open the door, ready to sob back into my pillow, when I saw a figure sprawled out on my bed. Raf.

I was so happy to see him that I couldn't even form proper sentences. 'Not in the men's,' was all I could manage.

'No,' he replied, smiling wolfishly. 'I don't spend all my time there, you know?'

I moved forward and I think my pale swollen face must have then been directly under the light as he seemed to register my horrific appearance and all mockery vanished.

'God, Noa, are you OK?' he whispered gently. 'I thought today would have been a great day for you. I mean these are some of your best subjects. I thought we could celebrate together. It all being over, I mean.'

I told him about my Chemistry fiasco and I could see worry lines form on his face and his eyebrows starting skulking just like Dad's. When he finally spoke it was with quiet determination.

'You're over-reacting Noa. You'll have done really well in the other sciences and Maths, you'll have extra percentage points in the bag so you'll still totally average 70 per cent. I'm not worried.' But his eyebrows didn't look so convinced.

'I've got to average 72 per cent, remember. And what if I don't? What if they take me away and that's it? I'll die some horrific death in some swamp. And I'll never get to see … lots of people again.'

'That's not going to happen,' Raf urged. 'I think I've passed and there's one thing I'm sure of and that's you're way smarter than me. You are massively smart, Noa. You'll get to stay, no doubt. And even if I fail, you'll stay and Jack can look after you.'

'But I don't want Jack,' the words were out of my mouth before I could stop them. 'I just want you.' And the brutal honesty of my words hit me. Despite everything he's done for me, despite the years he's been my best friend, if it comes down to a choice, I choose Raf.

And then in that same moment, I saw Raf's face fall and heard the door to the dorm slam. On autopilot I ran to the door, opened it and just disappearing round the bend at the end of the corridor, I saw a huge frame and a beacon of carrot-red hair.

I'm like some massively unlucky charm. Do not approach unless you're at least touching wood and chucking salt over your left shoulder.

We were woken by the sirens at 3am, those of us that had gone to sleep. No one understood what was going on. Everyone in my dorm thought it was probably a fire drill, the sort we have at school every six months, where we have to file out onto the playing field at the back and get counted while the lamest, keenest students in yellow jackets check for the non-existent source of the non-existent flames.

We weren't left to think for long though. The door to the dorm was thrown open with a bang as the handle crashed into the cupboard behind. Filling the entire doorframe was a massive guard who ordered us to follow him in silence. He'd already collected a long line of students, most of whom I recognised from Hollets, and he propelled us towards the exam hall, picking up more and more students on route. Down other corridors we glimpsed similar processions and even saw one girl getting thrown against a wall by a guard for some unseen offence. It was feeling less and less like a fire drill and more and more like a military crackdown. Even though we'd been ordered to be silent, different theories were being whispered up and down the line until just one dominated.

There was a runner.

Helena in Mr Forbes class's cousin had apparently had this happen to her. The siren meant someone had been seen breaking out of the Waiting Place and it only stopped when the fugitive had been caught by the guards or their dogs or shot resisting capture. Sometimes, the whispers gleefully asserted, the runner had to be shot because they'd been so badly mangled by the dogs. Either way, the siren normally stopped in less than twenty minutes.

'But how could anyone get out?' I whispered to the guy in front of me. 'This place is like a prison.' My question was whispered up the line and an answer duly returned.

'There's a flat roof you can reach from the first floor. From that you can climb over barbed wire and jump down over the wall. It's a ten-foot drop though. You'd probably break your legs.'

Inside the exam hall, we were herded into groups according to school. We were so tightly crammed it was impossible to see beyond the first circle of faces so I couldn't seek out the comfort I craved from Raf, or Jack for that matter, not that he'd probably feel like comforting me. In a robotic monotone our guard began to read out names and check them off against this long list. When it was your turn you had to answer and go up to a screen and press your fingertip onto the touch-pad to prove your identity. So no one could go up twice to cover for the runner. The list was alphabetical. I answered mechanically to Noa Blake and touched the screen. Although I obviously am and always have been Noa Blake, I still had a moment of blind panic when I touched the screen and there was a fraction of a second delay before the little circular light turned from red to green. 'Raf Ferris' was answered by a 'yes' and my stomach double-flipped in relief. My mind kind of zoned out for the rest of the Fs to Ls. Then the guard called, 'Jack Munro', and there was silence followed by a frantic low-level buzz of speculation. 'Jack Munro,' the guard called again. Again there was no reply and the buzz grew louder. The guard grabbed the radio from his jacket. 'We have the runner. The runner is Jack Munro. I repeat Jack Munro.'

No one could believe Jack had run. No one apart from me and Raf anyway. To me it all made horrific, logical sense. Jack, who cared more about me passing than him, who'd sheltered and protected me all the way to this hellish place, now running away, throwing it all away because I'm a horrible selfish user. All my mind could do was replay over and over again the image of Jack running;

running down the corridor; running away from me; and my mouth opening and saying over and over, 'But I don't want Jack, I don't want Jack.'

Raf managed to worm his way through the knot of students to hold my hand, but for once I got no warmth from it. His touch just intensified my guilt.

And as Jack's 'best friend', everyone came to ask me why I thought he'd done it. After the exams, they all thought he'd been smiling, relatively happy, not acting like someone who'd definitely failed and was going to take desperate measures.

And then the siren stopped. Radios crackled and the guards started marching us back to our dorms. No word on Jack. I begged one guard to at least tell me if Jack was alive or dead, but he acted like I didn't exist. 'Please!' I tugged on his arm, but then he hit me so hard that I was on the ground, tasting metallic blood for the second time in my life.

On the way back to the dorms I saw various students passing money to Hugo. 'What's going on?' I asked Bernard who was in front of me. 'Sweepstake,' Bernard replied. Bernard mistook my scowl for confusion. 'On how long it'd be till they got him, I mean,' he explained. 'Hugo won, of course.' Then, I think out of some emotionally inept attempt at comfort, he said, 'It was twenty-three minutes. Jack did well.'

Bastards. Complete utter bastards.

Results Day. In ten minutes I find out whether I've passed or failed.

At precisely 11am the guards will herd us back into the exam hall to get our results. According to Helena, who seems to know more than anyone else about this place, the hall will be split into three by floor to ceiling bars. One massive cage that everyone gets put in to start with, with a raised stage at the far end. Two doors off the stage each leading to a smaller cage.

Everyone's name is called out in turn followed by your percentage. You have to go forward, fingerprint identify yourself and either a green or red light shines. Then a guard opens the door to the relevant smaller cage.

Like some sick game-show host.

Green light – right-hand door – *congratulations, you're a winner, your prize is: Life!*

Red light – left-hand door – *bad luck this time, you're a Fish. But here's a consolation prize of a mosquito net and some iodine tablets.*

There are loads of extra guards with massive guns to prevent you trying to escape after the announcement or 'do a Jack' as every freakoid is now calling it.

There's still no word on Jack. Raf says, 'No news is good news,' but we both know he's just trying to cheer me up as that's a lame saying that means nothing. Everyone's convinced he's dead. Because surely they'd tell us if he was still alive. Wouldn't he be allowed visitors or something? But maybe not. A regime that hunts down teenagers with dogs probably isn't that up on human rights.

Any sort of noise and I think the guards are here already. I think I'm going to be sick. After Jack's escape, I'd kind of forgotten that I've most likely failed. I remember now though. Oh God, I remember pretty damn clearly.

The results were boomed out of loudspeakers as soon as we were all rammed into the large holding cage. The air was charged as the first result came. 'Finn Abbott … 73 per cent.' I didn't know him. He was from another school and too far away for me to see if he had a Node or not. He screamed with joy, leapt onto the stage, pressed his finger to the machine and swaggered into the right-hand cage.

Tom Adams, a niceish Norm from the other class was the first Red light. He started crying hysterically on the stage and a puddle of pee formed at his feet. Everyone backed away from the stage and there were cries as someone got knocked over. We felt terrible for Tom. But it was like we HAD to get away from him. Like failure might be catching. The guards hit him with a baton and made him walk through the door into the left-hand cage.

'Please let me pass, please let me pass.' I chanted the mantra over and over under my breath.

Being 'Blake,' I didn't have to wait long. 'Noa Blake.' When I reached the stage and heard '76 per cent' and the green light shone, I actually puked a little bit in my mouth from sheer relief. I wasn't going to be sent to die. I wasn't going to kill my parents.

From then on there was this sort of sound-orgy of air-punching 'Yes!!!' and howls of 'No!!'. Raf passed too and I sent up a massive prayer of thanks. As he entered the right-hand cage and stood next to me, I clutched his hand and left red marks I was gripping so hard. Our eyes met and he mouthed, 'I love you!' and I was so high on the moment that I lost all my rubbish inhibitions and mouthed, 'I love you too!' right back at him.

And then came the most shocking words of the day, 'Jack Munro'.

That confirmed it. Jack was alive.

Two guards marched towards the stage carrying, or rather dragging, Jack between them. Jack, with two black eyes and a broken leg. Jack, beaten and humbled but still Jack, my Jack.

'71 per cent,' the loudspeaker announced and I literally shouted with joy. Tears started streaming down my face. He'd managed the impossible. Jack had actually passed the

TAA!!! I felt like we'd all been given a second chance. That there was some sort of justice in the world after all.

That's when the red light shone. I choked back my disbelief. But he'd got 71 per cent. 'They can't do this. How can then do this?' I whispered in rage to Raf. And then the disembodied voice of the loudspeaker continued, 'Disqualified for attempted escape'.

The guards unceremoniously dumped Jack in the left-hand cage.

'No!' I howled.

A guard approached. 'Quiet! Or you'll be in there yourself,' he spat. But that wasn't the voice that stopped me.

'Noa, leave it!' It was Jack from the other side of the bars. Jack, protecting me still. Even after everything. Raf tactfully backed away.

'Oh, God,' was all I could manage, overwhelmed by the unfairness of it all. 'I'm so sorry Jack, it's all my fault. I did this to you.'

'It's not, Noa,' Jack replied sadly. 'I did this to myself. I got angry and acted stupid like normal. Wish I'd just punched something – escaping was maybe a step too far.' His attempts at humour just made my heart hurt more. He picked up on it, like he always does, like there was some form of telepathy between us. 'I love you Noa. We both know that. But you don't owe it to me to love me back. I get that now. So look after yourself, OK? It's not your fault. It's mine.'

I started crying openly and Jack tried to pretend that he wasn't too.

But beneath my tears I felt some of that steel that I must have inherited from Mum.

A guard dragged me away from the bars and Jack and back to the middle of the cage.

Raf wrapped me in his arms. Surrounding me in comfort. In a safety where I could have happily stayed forever. But I wasn't going to.

I looked up into Raf's eyes. 'I don't know how or anything, but I'm going to the Wetlands to get him out. You know that, don't you?'

'I thought you might.' He looked at me, trying to work out if there was any doubt in my mind. There wasn't. 'OK. Just let me know when we leave.'

And then he squeezed my hand so hard that he left red marks and I knew that he meant it.

Acknowledgements

Huge thanks to my husband, without whose constant encouragement I would never have made it beyond two thousand words. Thanks to Nina Duckworth, Eirlys Bellin, Sammy Mennell and Sarah Brodie for their invaluable feedback on the first draft. Thanks to my agent, Rupert Heath, for taking on an unknown and finding a home for my first novel. Thanks to Penny and Janet at Firefly for their unswerving faith and enthusiasm and to Megan Farr and Jennie Scott for their tireless PR efforts. Thanks to Jo Nicholls and Seana Johansson-Keys and everyone else who helped select the fabulous cover. And finally, thanks to my parents and thanks to my old schools for being nothing like those in The Territory.

Sarah Govett read law at Trinity College, Oxford. After qualifying as a solicitor, she set up her own tutoring agency. Sarah has also written for children's television.

She has two young children and lives in London.

Out Now

Book Two

The Territory, Escape

The exams are over, but the struggle is just beginning...

£7.99

ISBN 978-1-910080-46-7

fireflypress.co.uk

Out Now

Book Three

The Territory, Truth

How far can you go and still be on the
right side...? The nail-biting conclusion
to the Territory series.

£7.99

ISBN 978-1-910080-70-2

fireflypress.co.uk